Malicious Mates

Raz Andrews

Big Smoke Books

Melbourne

Published by Big Smoke Books.

ISBN 978-0-6485475-1-8

Raz Andrews VIR List

Add yourself to the VIR List to receive the free visual companion booklet, *Maps of Malicious Mates*. Details can be found at the end of the novel.

For the fine who went before

Contents

Chapter 1

Exegesis Drinking

'Crocodiles are easy. They try to kill and eat you. People are harder. Sometimes they pretend to be your friend first.'
Steve Irwin, *d. 2006.*

My boss is my nightmare. At this hour on a Friday night, a little past five, I should be on my tram home for a quiet night in with Chelsea. But instead, I'm seated at the boardroom table in the corner of our open plan office, surrounded by all four of my workmates. From our vantage point on the fourteenth floor, I watch my last hope of natural light slip away behind the towering skyscrapers that rise to form Melbourne's skyline.

Today is the shortest day of the year.

Darkness has arrived at its earliest.

Judging by the three empties next to my boss, and the half-full in his hand, he's been smashing beers hard this last hour. In celebration of arriving at an age I estimate to be somewhere deep in his forties. This was his idea, these birthday drinks. As he mentioned to us earlier in the week: a chance to get to know each other, to come closer as a team. An ambitious statement based on his assumption that we'll like what we find in each other when we do.

'To tonight!' my boss announces, rising from his seat.

Five green bottles attached to outstretched arms meet in the middle of the table for a cascade of clinks.

'Sorry I'm late, boys,' I say. 'Complication with the Cockburn account.'

Didn't happen.

In truth, I wanted to give the others a healthy head-start on the piss in hope they'd be drunk enough not to notice my slightly slower drinking pace. Chelsea's hours at the hospital florist have been all over the place of late, and tomorrow is our first day off together in some time. I'd rather not ruin it, then, by nursing an introvert-inducing hangover as I drip beer sweats over my eggs Benedict. My investment in tonight's celebration is solely to keep a close eye on Ed Best, whose large snout keeps coming at me from across the boardroom table. The team leader position has been recently vacated, and I don't want him snaking me for the gig by manipulating my boss between rounds of Chartreuse shots. My plan is to hang around long enough that when my boss wakes up in bed tomorrow, with a burger on his pillow and a sock on his dick, he'll remember that I was here, but he won't remember how early I left. I'll add two hours to the truth on Monday. This should be enough to maintain my edge over Ed. As for the others, Will Crowther's too young and Rick Fitzpatrick's accent too rural for either to be considered seriously for the role.

As far as I'm concerned.

Though, it is possible recruitment hasn't been at the top of my boss's mind of late. He hasn't spoken directly of it to me, but Ed Best whispered in my ear at the urinal a few days ago that my boss was binned by his wife a couple of weeks back after he confronted her about an affair she was having with her personal trainer. Goes a long way to explain the ferocity of my boss's drinking tonight. A gym would seem a logical place for his wife to conduct her side hustle because my boss certainly hasn't stepped inside one for at least a decade. Our boardroom table hides most of his guts that spill over a chafing belt. Above that, a light blue shirt hangs off two decimated shoulders, and deep underarm sweat patches are illuminated by the fluorescents every time he raises beer to lips.

'Where's good to go tonight, boys?' my boss slurs.

I know where's terrible. I could throw him a hundred names within a five-minute walk of the foyer doors.

'Gin Den's not bad,' I offer the table. 'Chill. Doesn't take too long to get—'

'No, Jackson!' Ed Best turns to my boss. 'What you want, Carl, is somewhere with a decent after-work crowd.'

My boss nods with so much aggression in his agreement that it unsettles me.

Ed continues, 'Psychopomp is where you want to be on a Friday.'

'I think I've been there before,' my boss says. 'Where's that again?'

'Near the corner of La Trobe and Russell.'

'Not sure if I have, then.'

'You would know if you had. You would know. *Fri Yay Happy Hour Cocktails till Ten*. Gets the girls in early. Struck luck there on frequent occasion,' Ed claims.

Rick Fitzpatrick—tipping sixty, the oldest at the table—chimes in with his piece, 'On the chase tonight, boys? You're lucky I'm out of the game.'

My boss once told me that Rick found his first girlfriend at forty-five and married her by forty-six. But still, that ring on Rick's wrinkled finger has messed with his mind long enough that he now believes the only thing stopping him from banging the chick of his choice in the piss-soaked shit booths of Psychopomp is some internal moral compass loosely tied to his wedding vows. My boss blatantly ignores Rick's delusional declaration and calls out to Will, a good looker in his early twenties, who's yet to fill out the shoulders of his suit jacket.

'Will, where do people your age—' my boss catches the creep in his voice. 'Any new bars that you've been to lately? That are good?'

'I sort of do more parties, than bars,' Will says, swallowing his words.

An ill silence follows, one Will thankfully resolves.

'There's a student bar near Melbourne Uni that we drink at sometimes.'

'That sounds good,' my boss says, taking a deep swig of his beer as his eyes dart around the table searching for votes of support.

'Everyone's kinda young there, though,' Will adds.

'Let me tell you something about *girls*, Will,' my boss says, pointing at him with an angry finger. 'Age means nothing. What they want is someone with confidence, someone who has their life together. Financially secure. Someone who knows what he wants and goes after it. Who takes control. Age means nothing.'

My boss nods to himself in approval of his own words, and Ed Best takes this as a cue to slap his hand hard on the boardroom table and yell out, 'Too right!' But the truth is, my boss is screwed. He just doesn't know it yet.

Chapter 2

Crow's Feet and Widow's Peaks

Our attention has drifted away from the boardroom table. We stand at the triple-glazed windows watching another rush hour protest play out on Swanston Street. From our vertigo view, we see cheaply constructed signs waving at us from the usual coalition crowd of young students and old eccentrics. On the opposing side: the police. Their cars parked on kerbs in disorderly fashion, flashing blue and red over the hundred or so riot officers assembling in the dark. I follow an old man, hunched, holding supermarket bags in each hand, hobbling across the street, weaving between all the chaos.

I've loosely followed the news on this recent growing tension, somewhat adopting Chelsea's intensifying interest in current affairs of late. Her nightly religious viewing: *The Sign of our Times with Nigel Lassiter.* The law in dispute is one that would legally allow federal authorities to use your phone to listen to you—without the need to establish reasonable cause. As if they weren't already. Yet these misdirected, idealistic protestors are trying to win favour for their cause by taking away our God-given right to get home without delay or hindrance on an icy cold, miserable Melbourne night. Stop me from getting where I need to go, and I'm against you.

The protests have been getting progressively more violent over the last few years, so the last slither of authoritarian tolerance is wearing thin. Especially since the killing a few months back. A CEO of a private debt-collection firm, contracted by the government to chase student loan defaulters, was assassinated after leaving work one night. Bludgeoned to death with his own briefcase; one of the more gruesome political protests of recent times.

With no batons battering bohemians just yet, we quickly lose interest and sit back down at the boardroom table to continue our attack on the bottle of whiskey, already three-quarters destroyed.

'That's the best thing about being single,' Ed Best spouts with a wink. 'When you go out, the night's like a blank canvas. You could end up anywhere. Wake up anywhere.'

'Handcuffed to a hospital bed,' I say. 'Or worse. Alone in your own.'

'What have you got on tomorrow, Jackson?' Ed asks. 'Whatever Chelsea's doing? Death that. Always doing what she wants. Trust me, mate, really dangerous.'

'At least I know where my next one's coming from,' I say. 'Tends to take the edge off things,' and I lean back in my leather boardroom chair to let my point rest.

'Big night ahead, Ed,' my boss pulls out of nowhere. 'You, me: the dream team.'

He reaches out his beer to meet Ed's, and their bottles collide loudly. But my boss's confidence is misplaced. When he goes out tonight, it won't matter the money he has in the bank. Or the house he'll soon only half own. It will all count for nothing. Nothing. My boss looks late forties at least, crow's feet kicking from both eyes, which isn't necessarily a problem in a dimly lit nightclub. He'll get some cover of darkness for that one. But his vicious widow's peak flecked with generous greys has no chance of escaping the dancefloor strobe. He needs to be in no doubt that it's carnage out there now and that all odds are firmly stacked against him at his age. When he goes out tonight, there won't be a girl over thirty in the club, and a majority will have yet to hit the quarter century. Even if he gets close enough to some girl's ear for her to hear whatever verbal bile he thinks will spark her interest, his game was already over well before the bouncer begrudgingly unclipped the red velvet rope. Because the cold hard truth is this: His competition isn't even at the bar. He's competing against the twenty guys she matched with the past week and some parasailing instructor she banged in Ibiza two years ago who might be coming to Australia at some stage sometime soon. He's competing against an up-and-coming Hip Hop artist she's following on socials who liked back one of her pics once, and most terrifying of all, a perfect guy who only exists in an incredibly hallucinogenic part of her imagination. And because I understand the reality of what my boss is about to face, it makes me savour the fact that I have Chelsea and I don't have to deal with any of this anymore. Those nights in pursuit with my mates. The binge drinking, drunk fighting, double crossing, backstabbing, lunch cutting, cock blocking, shoplifting, ride soiling.

All that ended six years ago, with her.

The orchestrator of my escape.

Chelsea.

It only takes a moment
To escape
What you feared you'd become

7

This is his reality. My boss being an aged forty-something of average societal standing, forces me to take girls in their twenties off the table straight away. Now he's having a crack at that thirty-plus age group. This comes with an even more intimidating set of challenges: passion for travel, love to laugh, over one-night stands, debt ridden, weakness for tattoos, mother to two beautiful boys, enjoys good food, no time for dickheads, heavily medicated, pick your poison. And on top of this extreme headwind my boss is up against, trapped in a vessel well past its prime, his biggest problem is this: The trust issues he'll carry from his recent marriage breakdown will destroy any new relationship long before it has a chance to stick.

My boss is my nightmare.

I can see him struggling to keep his double chin off his chest as he fights the inevitable tiredness chasing him down, a permanent plague of his age. He puts both hands on the table, hoists himself from his chair with a deep guttural groan, and staggers off to the men's room. My phone hums in my pocket and I pull it out. It's a message from Chelsea that reads a little odd.

'What time will you be home? We need to talk.'

The sterility of her phrasing concerns me.

Chapter 3

Never Never Land

My boss is taking his time in the men's room. I imagine his extended toilet break is due to his aged colon refusing to release the remnants of a week's worth of microwave dinners that he ate off his lap alone, tears as condiments.

In his absence, the chat has descended into some sort of sordid confessional. Rick Fitzpatrick is telling a story from his younger years when he thought he had caught herpes off a public toilet seat, so he went to the doctor and was instead diagnosed with over-wanking. Rick's story ends with a prescription for steroid cream and stern advice from the doctor to be gentler on himself.

'Tell me that's not a true story,' I say as I walk to the kitchen for more beers.

As far as I'm concerned, not one person is close to normal at work. Except possibly young Will Crowther. Though, I'm certain he'll mature into an insanity with time. Almost inevitable if he racks up enough hours within these walls. We're a small team specialising in bespoke life insurance policies for the top end of town. Our clients: mostly tyrannical boomers craving financial immortality so to ensure the privileged survival of their spoilt spawn. There used to be six of us. That was before

Melanie Eve, our former team leader, unexpectedly quit last month. Old Rick Fitzpatrick muttered to me at the hand basins, not long after she left, that he reckoned my boss cracked on to her hard during the death throes of his dissolving marriage, and it was these unwanted advances that prompted her seemingly spontaneous resignation.

My boss returns from the men's room and slumps back into his chair as Ed Best wraps up another conquest story.

'… and before I left her yacht, I made it very clear that in no way whatsoever was I looking for any sort of girlfriend.'

'How hot was she?' Rick asks, chomping on the bait.

'Better than I ought to be getting,' Ed says. 'Way better!'

Conveniently, this leaves it up to individual interpretation as to what Ed *should* be getting. His stories sit a sack hair on the inside of plausible, but I doubt any are true. He's underestimated my experience, Ed has. I learnt a lot in the field before I met Chelsea. I can see right through the drunken bravado spilling from his beaked nosed, beady eyed face—an unfortunate ensemble saved only by his generous height. Ed's tactic is to get the inside running for the team leader promotion by positioning himself as some sort of ultimate wingman as my boss attempts to rebuild his shattered life. But my boss needs to know this: Ed Best is not his ally, he's his rival.

He's been quiet since his return, my boss has. He's slumped at the head of the boardroom table, his vacant eyes staring down at the empty whiskey glass resting in his right hand. I expect he's having traumatic flashbacks of perfectly formed glutes pounding his marital bed to a metronomic beat.

One, two, three, four.

Two, two, three, four.

Ed Best gets up to drain his bladder, and once he's out of earshot, I lean into the table and drop my emotional Manhattan Project.

'For a bloke that looks like something Jim Henson chucked in a skip, Ed goes quite well with the ladies. Cops his unfair share of roots, that's for certain. The girl from the yacht, the model from the weekend before…'

And I hit the kill switch.

'Melanie Eve.'

Straight away my boss's chin rises from his chest. I lean back in my chair and hold up my hands in defence, as if I've said too much. But I haven't. All I've done is laid an idea down on the table and allowed those sitting around it to decide their truth. Old Rick Fitzpatrick runs with it, waving a recollecting finger.

'I knew it. I fucken knew it, that sly cunt. Saw them get in the same ride together after the national conference.'

We hear the gentle swing of the men's room door, and our conversation ceases immediately. Ed Best sits down with a smile and a sigh of urethral relief.

'What I miss?' he asks.

My boss gets up from his seat without making eye contact with Ed or anyone and retires to the men's room once more.

Under the table, I reply to Chelsea.

'Hey. Leaving soon. X.'

We finish the bottle of whiskey and start another. I feel I should go soon. One more celebratory drink for a job done well. Leave in ten or so. Maybe pump up my boss a bit when he gets back from the shitters. Chuck the hose down Ed's throat some more. That's what my boss once told me I should to do to a drowning man.

Corporate analogy.

The men's room door swings open with enough violence that we all turn to look. Will Crowther's blood-drained face leans out and calls to us.

'Help! I need some help in here!'

For fuck's sake.

Chapter 4

Anarchic Winds

The smell of vomit stings my eyes. Will walks us to the far cubicle of three. The door is locked red to occupied. Rick drops to the floor with a coarse exhale reflective of his age and yells out underneath the door.

'Carl. You okay in there? Carl?'

Unresponsive.

As the only one with any upper body strength to speak of, I pull myself up over the top of the cubicle. In my second or two of held view, I see a mess of crumpled human sprawled on the floor, limbs pointing in possessed directions.

> People ask you how your dad died
> He had an epileptic fit
> Hit his head on the bathroom tiles
> You say

'Give me a boost,' I tell the others. Their collective hands help me over the cubicle wall, and I land heavily on my boss's foot. His pants and undies are around his ankles, and projectile shit is splattered across the toilet seat that he's now using as a pillow. Streams of chunder work their way down his light blue shirt and curdle in his unkempt pubes. I try to look anywhere but his bits. Anywhere. He's managed to smash his head against the cubicle wall too, as there's a big bloody smear near the toilet paper dispenser and a whole lot more of it matted in his hair.

'Check for a pulse!' Rick yells out from under the door.

But I'm hesitant to get blood, or sick, or shit, on my white shirt. In a one-two beat, my boss dry retches, then farts, as if his bodily gases can't endure another moment in his company either. Thankfully, with his life now established, my white shirt is saved. I crudely manoeuvre his crumpled body with the heel of my foot to allow the cubicle door to swing open inwards. On seeing the full state-of-affairs, Rick addresses us in a somewhat serious tone.

'You guys go. I'll handle this.'

'You sure, Rick?' Will asks.

'Yes, go, go. Nothing to see here.'

'Fuck this,' Ed blasts. 'I had a quiet night in last night, in anticipation for tonight.'

'You can still go out,' Rick says.

'Not on *my* fucken coin, I'm not,' and Ed gestures his huge nose down towards my coma'd boss.

'Jesus Christ,' Rick lowers himself onto his one good knee and fishes in my boss's pocket for his wallet. There's a bit of vomit near the opening, so he has to pick at it carefully with his finger and thumb until the wallet slides free. Rick flicks it open, takes out the corporate credit card, and hands it up to Ed.

'Leave, you lot,' Rick orders. 'I'll clean up this mess.'

'Thanks,' Ed says, sliding the card into his wallet.

****

I press G in the lift and try my best to forget the sight of my boss's wrinkly dick and sack. And I try to forget that as we walked out of the men's room, my boss called out for his wife, 'Audrey.'

We stand in silence while the floors fall, Ed, Will, and I, until Will says, 'Fuck me,' under his breath. It's the first time I've ever heard him swear. I can tell by the way Ed's bouncing his head that he's keen to keep the night going, but I've had about all I can take of this lot for one evening. And with career advancement opportunities over, all I care about now is getting home to my couch, the heater, and my peppermint tea.

To where I'd rather be.

Chelsea.

The foyer doors open, and the cold of the night takes a swing at my face. My chest tightens, and my hands plunge heavy into my coat pockets. We walk out into the wind, and I immediately realise that free societal debate has taken a turn for the worse while we were preoccupied with the shat pants of my boss. Venomous voices echo between skyscrapers. Across the street, angry flames lick at an upturned cop car. Dark plumes pour skywards from the charring chassis, catching in the cold wind and swirling with the green tear-gun gas as they both rise together towards the starless night sky. Through the smoke, I sight gas-masked riot police walking up Swanston in arrow formation. The rioters retreat in disorder, throwing whatever the street hands them at the shields and batons in pursuit. The swarm of scattered feet have created an endless queue of trams held up outside the State Library.

'Every fucken Friday,' I sigh.

My frustration fuelled by the fact that it's over an hour back to my apartment by foot and near on impossible to find a ride amongst all this chaos.

It starts spitting. Through the crowd, in tiny little flashes, I think I see Chelsea. I see a dark silhouette of a girl holding a black and white polka dot umbrella and walking alongside a taller man. But before I can tell if it's her for certain, she's gone.

'Alright, no excuses now, boys,' Ed Best says. 'Trams aren't moving anytime soon. Psychopomp it is. Follow me.'

Chapter 5

Angry Men

The storefront overhang protects us from the heavying rain. We climb the gradient of La Trobe Street, following behind Ed, who's walking everywhere but a straight line. All four limbs flail from their joint sockets as he tacks left and right across the footpath.

'Hurry the fuck up!' Ed shouts at us over his shoulder. 'There's a hot bartender who works there some Fridays. If we get there too late, it'll get too busy to talk to her.'

Will and I are following a couple of metres behind, walking dead into the ice wind and struggling to keep pace with Ed's drunken charge forth.

'The protestors go hard at it,' Will says, his words steaming in the night air.

'Please, Will,' I say. 'You know how these things start, don't you? Some girl gets an idea to stage a protest. She sends out the word to round up the troops. A guy who likes the girl joins, and she asks him to bring as many people as possible. He sends the call out, and a couple of girls who like the guy join, or some guy who likes the guy joins. It's not a political movement, it's a pyramid scheme of unrequited love.'

'Hurry up, ya fucks!' Ed yells from nearly a block away.

'*That's* why they're angry, Will,' I say.

The last fragments of rioters are running up La Trobe Street between the congested traffic; cars and buses packed with commuters desperate to get to their haven of home. Every vehicle jostling with each other for the slightest gap in a lane, cutting each other off with aggressive acceleration and sudden breaking. An armed squad of four riot officers runs past us. Full SWAT uniform, automatic rifles pointed at the pavement. We're ignored, of course. Our white business shirts, ties, and winter long coats identifying us as non-threatening civilians.

You know

There's no line at the red rope and carpet of Psychopomp, yet Ed is still waving his hand at us to hurry up. He ushers us aggressively to the front door and shoves us both in the back to make sure we go in before him. As if he's scared we'd ghost him if he went in first himself. As if it's happened to him before. I walk in, pay my cover, get my stamp. Will walks in, pays his cover, gets his stamp. Ed walks in and gets a firm hand on his shoulder.

'How much you had to drink tonight, mate?' a bouncer with a goatee asks.

'Ah, fuck! Really? Seriously?' Ed says.

Will and I are hovering around the foyer area. The bouncer throws us a 'fuck off inside' with a rather flamboyant flick of his wrist. We follow his suggestion and leave Ed alone to argue his sobriety.

This place is dead. Sticky underfoot and sour smelling, its lack of cleanliness suggests the owners must have considerable sway over the council health board. There's only one bartender. A fat bloke in a black T-shirt. Other than that, just a guy and a girl sitting in a booth in the corner. She's attractive, in a suburban-bar bikini contest sort of way. He's got one of the angriest faces I've seen in a long time. A short, shaven head, face-tatted mug who I'm near certain sneered at me when I first walked in. And while I'd rather be home than here right now, the one upside of the riot is that I can finally see firsthand how vast the chasm is between Ed's claims and his reality, *if* he manages to talk his way past the bouncer.

I go to the bar, and I'm forced to order pints from the tap because this place is so fucken heathen it doesn't even sell one brand of green-bottled beer. I walk back to our bar leaner with a frothed-up pint in each hand. I feel Face Tatt's eyes follow me across the empty dancefloor that's lit up by flowing kaleidoscope lights. I don't return eye contact. No point in trouble. Not for someone like me. Nothing for me to prove to anyone tonight. Though, I'll admit it's somewhat disconcerting when a bloke, half a foot shorter than you, tells you confidently with just a glance that he'd happily stomp out your teeth if the wind were to swing that way.

'You know Ned Kelly was hung a couple of doors up?' Will says.

I hand him his pint.

'Hanged,' I say.

****

'Talk my way out of any situation and into any bed,' Ed says as he rocks up with a pint in hand. He slurps the foam, surveys the room, and winces. Either at how foul the tap beer tastes or how empty the bar is. Or quite possibly both. It's even quieter now than when we first walked in. The girl in the booth is sitting alone. About ten minutes ago, I saw Face Tatt get up in a hurry and go through a set of swinging doors off to the side of the bar.

'Well, there ya go, Ed,' I tip my pint towards the girl. 'All by herself. Go on, mate. Show us how it's done, then.'

Ed rolls his neck, takes a big sip, wipes his mouth with the back of his hand, and starts his strut over to her.

Chapter 6

Mazel Tov!

Ed's reading her palm now. He's sitting next to the girl in the booth, up close, his slender index finger delicately tracing the details of her future. She keeps looking over Ed's shoulder, her eyes searching for the beast out back. Pop music spills through the distorting sound system, telling me how good my night is going to be.

WOOHOO!

And Ed's up, punching the air and spilling his beer. He's tugging at her arm, pleading for her to get up and dance with him. She's laughing but shaking her head 'no.' Ed looks over to us, fearful that he's failing in our eyes. His resolve strengthens. He tugs on her arm again, harder, and she rises to her feet with an eye-rolling sigh and a resigned smile. Ed twirls her on the dancefloor. There ya go, mate! Another spin in the other direction now.

MAZEL TOV!

And Face Tatt walks up behind Ed and slams a half-drunk pint into the back of his head. Ed stumbles. His long legs twist under him, but he manages to keep his feet. I get up off my stool. Not to help. But to give the illusion I considered it.

'Fuck,' Ed reaches for the back of his head. His hand

returns covered in blood. Face Tatt hasn't said anything. He's just pacing back and forth, breathing hard through his nostrils, chest puffed out.

'Shannon, don't,' the girl says. 'Please, Shannon. Let it go this time.'

The bouncer with the goatee charges past us. He runs straight up to Ed, grabs him in a headlock, and marches him towards the front door.

'What the fuck, cunt?' Ed chokes out from the bouncer's hold. 'It was him who hit me! He hit me!'

Ed starts dragging his feet, an infant throwing a temper tantrum in a supermarket aisle.

'Don't fight it,' the bouncer says between gritted teeth as they pass our leaner. 'Don't fight it.'

'He hit me, you fucken pig imposter!'

'I'm saving you from yourself, mate. Trust me.'

I push my dregs away, 'I'm done with this place. Down your drink, Will.'

I pick up Ed's coat, and Will sculls the rest of pint in one, and we follow the scuffle outside to the Antarctic cold.

****

'For fuck's sake!' Ed, now released from the bouncer's hold, throws his head back at the sight of twenty or so short hemmed sequined dresses lining up around the corner to get into Psychopomp. The traffic is still angry, stabbing horns at each other, but at least the rain has stopped for now. Generous droplets of blood collect on the back of Ed's white shirt. I feel my point has been made, so I grab his arm.

'C'mon, mate. Let's find another bar,' I say. 'One with a bit more of a dancefloor.'

Ed bats away my arm with a clenched fist, 'Fuck off, Jackson,' and turns to the bouncer, pulling back his shirt cuff to show him the stamp on his wrist. 'Paid my cover, cunt. Let me back in.'

'Get the fuck out of here, mate,' the bouncer replies.

Ed takes out my boss's corporate credit card and flashes it in the face of the bouncer, 'Was gonna drop a couple of grand behind the bar tonight, you fucken sack-of-shit. Bet ya boss won't be happy when he finds out how much takings you just threw out the door.'

'He drove a glass into the back of your head. I suspect he'll forgive me for this specific disservice. Now get your tumour snout the fuck out my face.'

The bouncer points his thick arm down Russell Street, but Ed gets up on his toes and starts pedalling fists. The bouncer walks towards him, unintimidated. Ed takes a loose swing. The bouncer ducks under it and counters with a barrage of right hooks, left hooks, and an uppercut, snapping Ed's head back and sending his long lanky legs staggering over the kerb edge and out onto the road. There's a loud bang, a screech of brakes, an even louder bang, and a gasp from the girls in the line. A big black people mover is stopped in the middle of the street. A girl further up is screaming. Ed's nowhere to be seen.

Chapter 7

Dyatlov

We're running up the street towards the screams. Will's keeping pace with me, hanging off my shoulder. We run past the black people mover stopped in the middle of the street. There's a young boy in the back, strapped into a car seat. He's of an age that I suspect would still be counted in months, and his eyes cry out to me as we pass. Even this little guy knows it's bad.

> You tell them the tiles were wet
> Your dad had a seizure
> Slipped and hit his head
> Say it enough times

In the driver's seat is a woman who I assume is the child's mother. She's still gripping the steering wheel, leaning over it, shaking, staring at the smashed windscreen that's too shattered for her to see through. The bonnets all crushed in too. Will and I continue to run up the street towards the screams. I pass a severed foot still in its sock. A fair distance further up, we see it. We smell it too. Smells like shit. We get closer. Will puts his hands on his knees and vomits. Ed's broken and seeping out onto the road. He's on his back, staring up at the dark clouds. His torso a burst sofa, his spine tearing out through his stomach. There's not one spot of white left on his business shirt.

Sirens, sirens.

'That's his guts, Jackson.'

'I know, Will.'

'That's his guts, right there.'

'Thank you, Will. Yes, I can see that, thank you very much.'

Will slides out of his winter coat and starts unbuttoning his shirt. A police car turns up. An officer with a shaven head and a trimmed beard gets out of the driver's side, and a younger officer, a girl, steps out from shotgun with her brown hair tied back underneath her police cap. They take one look at Ed and head to the boot of their car where they snap on blue rubber gloves. They return and stand over him, one on either side, their hands on their hips.

'Where's the foot?' the bearded officer seems to ask Ed's bloody stump.

'Down that way,' I point.

'Right on,' he says. He turns to his partner, the girl, 'If you go grab the foot, I'll take care of this mess here.'

My sack starts to tingle at the sight I'm taking in. Bone, skin, pale face, the rain starting to fall across the street lights, splattered brains, rubberneckers, innards, the gathering crowd, the officer talking into his radio.

'Melbourne 318. We need an ambulance. We're on the corner of La Trobe and Russell. Got a male hit by a car. Clearly deceased. Please notify the coroner, we'll preserve the scene for now.'

The cop shakes his head as he surveys the scene at his feet.

'Anyone know this guy?'

'Yeah, I do,' I say.

'A friend of yours?'

'A workmate.'

'That'll do.'

The cop straddles Ed with a foot either side of his torso and bends down and empties Ed's pockets. He walks towards me and hands me a set of keys, a phone, and a wallet.

'Before some arsehole steals it,' he says. 'Get it to who it needs to go to.'

He puts on his paper rebreather mask, gets down on his hands and knees, and starts gathering the bloody chowder on the street. Big circling sweeps of his blue rubber gloves. Clean up in aisle five. His partner returns holding a clear plastic bag with the foot inside.

'Someone nicked off with the shoe already,' she says, dropping the bag next to Ed's head, and they cover the entirety of it with a bright blue tarp.

Will's down to his undies now.

****

More cops have arrived. Some talking to the bouncer, others standing around the smashed-up people mover. One of the cops, a tallish bloke, bounces the young boy on his hip, trying to cheer him up a little bit. The line to Psychopomp is longer and the rain heavier. An ambulance officer chases a naked Will up the street. She's holding a tin foil blanket that flails behind her like a cape in the wind.

Time for home, I think.

I walk back down to Swanston Street, and the riot appears to have subsided. My tram comes along, and I board near the back where there are plenty of empty seats. It's one of those new ones that has a solid heating system installed, so it's surprisingly pleasant. Out the window, the passing streetlights illuminate the Elms lining St Kilda Road, barely holding on to the last of their leaves. A whole continent of evergreens and some cunt plants all deciduous. I open Ed's wallet, take out the corporate credit card, and slide it inside my own.

Chapter 8

Halitosis Neurosis

The shower bites hot. I turn it up further, until I'm immersed in a cloud of steam. Chelsea always keeps our bathroom well stocked. She knows a lot about these types of things. I have a choice of two body washes: Geranium and Rosewood or Lemon Myrtle and Goats Milk. I go with the latter. A full body dousing. I also put some Heavenly Vanilla shower crème on this pink sponge thing and run it over my shoulders. There's some new shampoo too. Coffee Beans and Organic Coconut Oil. I squeeze out a generous serve and run it through my hair, pits, and pubes.

> Chelsea asked you who found him
> You told her the cleaner
> She found him on the bathroom floor
> Say it enough times

Chelsea's in bed, reading a book. *Shantaram.* She's reading it off her knees, resting her back against all the pillows and cushions that are piled up against the headboard. Her flowing blond hair falls down to frame her glasses. She's wearing pink polka dot pyjamas and she looks beautiful. I slide between the gold satin sheets and bury my face in the soft of her shoulder. She smells like lavender. It's this expensive balm thing she puts on just before she gets into bed. I get into it myself every now and then. Helps you get off to sleep quicker, it claims.

'Why didn't you stay with Will?' Chelsea asks.

'I would've just got in the way,' I say. 'He'll be fine. The ambulance people know what they're doing.'

'I hope so,' she says.

Chelsea switches off the bedside lamp, and the room falls into darkness.

A moment.

You know

'What did you want to talk about?' I whisper.

'You've had a big night,' she says, her voice drifting towards sleep. 'We'll talk tomorrow.'

'What is it?' I say. 'Chelsea?'

A moment.

You've known the answer
All night

'I've been thinking about us. I've been thinking…'

'You've been thinking?'

A moment.

'Of doing my own thing.'

It only takes a moment
To become
What you thought you'd escaped

I hold my hands over my face and fall into a paralysis.

A silent room.

A moment.

'Say something, Jackson.'

I can't.

Chelsea turns the bedside lamp on.

'Say something, please.'

I can't.

'I'm sorry, Jackson. I'm so, so sorry. I just don't feel what I did anymore. I can't—' her voice breaks, 'I can't help what I feel.'

> And you're old
> The brothel receptionist
> Hands you the card of her dental hygienist
> And tells you that you need to fix your breath
> Before you're allowed back

'Six years,' I say from under my hands.

'I'm sorry, Jackson. I just feel it in my gut. I need to do what's right for me.'

> And you're limping
> Towards the tinned food section
> Your dressing from the surgery is leaking
> And the pain killers have worn off
> But you haven't eaten all day

'Who's going to look after you?' I ask, my voice as soft as I've ever heard.

'I'm going to look after me,' she says.

And the doctors tell you
There's nothing more they can do for you
Do you have a friend or family member you can be with
Tonight?
You lie and say yes

I remove my hands from my face, and I see a large tear roll down her cheek. In this twisted moment, I feel torn to comfort her.

'I'm so sorry, Jackson,' and she rolls towards me and tries to put her arms around me. I turn away and get out of bed and start grabbing at some clothes. A pair of jeans, a T-shirt, a hoody. I pull my phone charger hard from the wall.

'Stay the night still, Jackson? Please?'

Tears well up in her eyes.

I can't sleep in a coffin.

I close the apartment door heavy behind me and press G in the lift. I'm waiting for her to yell out, waiting for her to run after me, waiting for her to tell me she's made a terrible mistake, that she just had a rough week at work. I'm waiting for her to walk up behind me, and for her arms to wrap around me, and for her to tell me that we'll sort it out. For her to tell me that we'll find a way through. That there's enough here not to throw six years away just like that. I'm waiting outside our apartment, and it starts to rain again. I'm waiting alone. And with nowhere to go, I start walking.

You knew it would end
This way

The streets are empty. The cold chews on my bones. From time to time, filled rides fly by, spraying water from their tyres.

I walk past closed cafés with chairs stacked on tables. Cafés that I know will be alive in a few hours' time, filled with couples putting their names down for the next available table. I walk some more. It's so late that the crossing buzzers sound the moment I hit the button. Red lights for phantom cars. But she doesn't call. And she doesn't come. And I know now, that it is done.

> You came home with your mother
> She told you to go to the bathroom
> Wash your hands before dinner
> She said

'Fuck you, ya cunt!' A guy leaning out the passenger's window of a passing ride flies the finger at me. I hunch my shoulders in the rain and watch the ride scream off into the distance. My hoody is waterlogged now. My teeth start to chatter. I have no option but to do it. Fuck, Chelsea, fuck. Something I have not done in two years. Could be three. I'm calling my best mate, Max.

Chapter 9

Faecal Treacle

I'm in foetal position, numb feet. The wooden venetian blinds are broken in enough places that they let in too much light to sleep. I'm freezing, trying to use the three tattered sofa cushions as both a pillow and a blanket. Max was too tired to stay up, so he left the key in the letter box and told me I could take the sofa. I heard he had bought a house a few months ago, the first of us to do so. I hadn't heard where. Until he messaged me the address last night.

'8 Windsor Close, Coburg.'

My ride dropped me off under a streetlight that cast a pale yellow over a wooden house with a small face, desperately gripping the side of a bank, next to the railway tracks. It was the only house on a cul-de-sac of factories and warehouses with broken windows. The yard was overgrown, weeds breaking through the wire fence that held a beat-up letterbox. It was into the dark depths of this letterbox that my hand had to fish between the snail-bitten junk mail and cobwebs, in a nervous search for the front door key.

And so here I lie. Curled up on this deformed sofa, split at the seams. It's a horrific lime green, and I'm near certain Max found it on the side of the road after it had caught some rain, so strong is the musty odour assaulting my sinuses. I cough up a tickle of spores from the back of my throat. The accompanying décor is a small television sitting inside a giant plywood cabinet, and a glass coffee table with a faded Men's Health magazine on it. 'Game Plan for Success,' is the cover title. And that's it. No artwork, no pot plants, no pottery. Nothing. Just tired walls, and wooden floors tattered in chaotic scratch marks. Max's foot in the property market has landed in a big steamy pile of shit. That's what this place smells like. Actual shit. And I'm starting to become genuinely concerned the odour is of human origin. I take out my phone and reread the message that greeted me when I first woke up this morning.

'You can pick up your stuff tomorrow. I'll be out 1–4. Leave your keys in the letterbox on your way out.'
'Can we talk?'

Unresponsive.

The front door bursts open. A violent crash. A gust of frozen air sprawls through the house. But nothing follows. I get up off the sofa to try to work out what it's all about. I turn in to the hallway, and my foot collects a tray of kitty litter, scattering its encrusted contents across the wooden floor. From the shadowy depths of the hallway, a door opens. Max emerges in a brown dressing gown and grey slippers. It seems there are two types of ageing. One where you mature and appear more distinguished. You grow into your looks. Clooney sipping coffee in Como. The other: you simply look like an extremely hungover version of your eighteen-year-old self. Max looks the latter. Like an anaemic first-year Uni student. Dark eyes, hunched shoulders, and a complexion that has long forgotten summer. He's so skinny, he almost looks tall; but he's not, he's always been the shortest of us. He still has his mousy blond hair though it's sickly in volume.

'Got a cat?' I ask Max.

'Had a cat. Till she chased a tyre.'

I look down at the crusty shit sprawled across the floor.

'When was that?'

'Bout a week back,' Max says. 'Maybe the week before. She's still in the bin down the side of the house. Keep forgetting to put her out on rubbish day.'

'You got a broom or something?'

'Nah, don't worry about it. I'll clean it up later. Been meaning to buy a vacuum.'

'Thought there was someone at the front door.'

'Nah, the fucken lock or latch thing is broken. Need to fix it one day. Fuck, just another fucken thing to do.'

Max closes the front door, shutting off the cold wind, and plays around with the lock and latch thing until it finally sticks. I follow him back into the living room. He rearranges the cushions back to normal and slumps into one end of the sofa. I take the other, and he punches the remote at the television. *The Word on the Street with Nigel Lassiter.* This is the cunt's Saturday morning show. He does a live broadcast from some street corner in the city every week. Goes up and asks Joe Public for their opinions. Makes them think they've got a voice for a moment, but he ends up doing most of the talking. Nigel Lassiter's mid-spiel, looking straight down the camera at us.

'… and to the police last night, you are possibly the most disgusting pieces of work to represent society. You should be ashamed of yourselves. People were protesting, peacefully I might add, and you deliberately antagonised those who want nothing more than to protect the rights of those less fortunate.'

Nigel Lassiter. He's all over fucken everything these days. Mid-fifties, ranga, with a beat-up face that looks like it caught the back wheel of a road train at some point. Still, has a hot wife in tow, trailing him by at least twenty years. She shat out their first foal about six months back, all over the fucken tabloids. I've seen him a few times in the flesh, Nigel Lassiter. He owns this big flash penthouse across the road from Carlton Gardens, not far from work, so we've occasionally crossed paths in the street and nodded to each other in passing.

'How'd ya sleep?' Max asks.

'Like Ledger sans Nyquil. Fucken freezing out here, mate. You should invest in some insulation or something.'

'There's a spare room next to mine. It might have been slightly warmer, but you would've had to have slept on the floor. Need to buy a bed for it sometime. Tell you what, the fucken shopping list never gets any shorter once you buy a house.'

'I was there. I saw. Police—you are bullies. You were acting like animals, and as a Victorian, I'm deeply ashamed of the continual and intentional provocation by our law enforcement officials.'

'Fight with the missus?' the prying cunt asks.

'Something like that,' I say. 'What about you? Got a girl on the go?'

I can tell he doesn't.

'Don't go out much. Not with the mortgage now. Trent does, though. Goes out all the fucken time, he does.'

'You still teaching?'

'Yeah.'

'Teaching what?'

'Social Studies,' he says. 'How's your job? Contents Insurance?'

'Life Insurance.'

'Yeah, that.'

'Yeah, it's alright. Is what it is. This joint come with a bathroom?'

'Yeah, mate. End of the hallway, second door on your left.'

I get up and follow his directions. Max calls out from the sofa, 'Welcome to a shower if you want. Only got the one towel, though. You could try the bathmat. See if it's dry.'

Max's bathroom's so bad, I can't picture it having ever been good. A scheme of beige with broken floor tiles exposing a rotting underfloor. The toilet might as well be in the bath, the space is that confined. The tub has a thick ring of green grime around it, and the pink shower curtain is littered with cultures of black mould. A brown bathmat—clearly waterlogged—lies in a heap on the tiles, and a grey towel is stuffed crudely between a rusty towel rack and the peeling wall. The toilet bowl is speckled with what can only be Max's shit. I aim at the specks, doing my part to clean up some of the mess. They put up a fierce fight, but I eventually start to dislodge the faecal treacle stuck to the inside of the bowl. Speck by speck. My phone hums in my pocket. Midstream, with help from my right hand, I take it out and read the message.

'To be honest, I feel it's too soon to talk, and I don't think it would achieve much at this point in time.'

Her words taunt me with their pretension. As if a nature hidden has now found full light. I flush my piss and drop the toilet seat with the tip of a finger nail, attempting to return some civility to the scene.

'Jesus Christ, Max,' I say as I slump back into the sofa. 'How does your shit grip to a slippery surface? What the fuck do you eat all day? Industrial adhesive?'

'Big Man Stew, mostly,' he says. 'Comes in a can. Heat it up on the stovetop. Got a mortgage now. Folks wrote me up a food budget a few weeks ago. Leaves little room for luxuries.'

I pick up the Men's Health magazine from the coffee table and start flicking through it.

'Also,' Max says, 'if you're planning to go out on the back lawn for any reason, remember to wear shoes. The junkies who live by the train tracks have made a game of throwing their old needles over my back fence. Need to write in to the council about that one day.'

Game Plan for Success. The worst thing I can do now is fake myself. Things won't work themselves out. Someone new won't come along when I least expect it. There will be no conversations in supermarket aisles or on public transport. Eyes won't meet across sweaty Bikram Yoga floors or across chopping boards at Sunday barbeques where I'm told to help Single Sally in the kitchen prepare her fucken Waldorf Salad. Dating devices are nothing more than an optic illusion of options and an easy way to waste six months of your life justifying your worth to vanilla strangers. Senses won't be come to. I know this. I accept this. Let me not kid myself about what I truly face. Burdened once again by constant chore. My only option is to go out. And when I'm tired and hungover, I need to pick myself up off the floor, pop some milk thistle, and drag myself out again. This is my only option to escape this hell right here: sitting with Max on this smelly lime sofa watching Nigel Fucken Lassiter.

'You got a car?' I ask him.

'Yes. Just.'

'Free tomorrow afternoon?'

The selfish sack-of-shit makes a sustained noise from the back of his throat, clearly fishing for an out—though we both know the truth is a given.

'At this stage,' he says.

'Good. I need you to help me with something.'

Chapter 10

The Black and White Polka Dot Umbrella

The black rubbish bag that Max is holding keeps tearing. We're at the apartment, in the bedroom that was once mine. Sunlight is streaming in through the window. It's one of those not-a-cloud-in-the-sky winter days, and I'd come close to calling it warm when the sun hits straight on.

'Max, fuck! I told you we should double bag it,' I say.

'These bags are fucken useless,' he says. 'The sides keep splitting.'

'Yeah, well, they were on special. Just double bag them and they'll fucken do.'

This is an in/out job.

Claim all that is mine: my clothes, my PlayStation, the air mattress, my sleeping bag, a pillow, my toothbrush; and get the hell out of this joint. I don't think about the other stuff. Things in frames and all that. I don't see it and I don't look at it. Look at it and I'll think about it. I focus only on the task at hand. The pure fundamentals of the present moment: Clearing out my clothes from the wardrobe and stuffing them in the bag that Max has now, thankfully, as per my instruction, finally double-bagged.

'So, where's Bones living now?' I ask.

'Belarus,' Max says.

'Where's that again? Off Spain or something?'

'Eastern Europe. Landlocked.'

There were four of us before her. Max, Trent, Bones, and myself. We met in our first year at Albert Park Grammar, but I wouldn't say commonality was our genesis. We were just four kids who found each other eating lunch on the tennis courts one day and ended up stuck with each other from there on in. Spent close to ten years putting up with all their shit, and by then, when she finally came along, I was more than fucken done with them. More than fucken done.

I unhook another jacket from its hanger and stuff it into the black rubbish bag Max is holding open for me with two outstretched arms.

'How'd Bones end up in Belarus?' I ask.

'Mate, it's stuff nightmares are made of.'

'Good, good. Start at the beginning, then. And don't leave anything out.'

'Okay,' he begins. 'Well, a few years ago, Bones was making an absolute killing in real estate. Made sure everyone knew about it too. Drove a shiny new white Mercedes off the lot once. Soon after that, he signed up to some elite dating agency. They tipped him into three dates in three weeks, and he went all out to impress. Thousand-dollar cufflinks, Michelin star restaurants. All that came of it, though, was three wide-armed hugs and one peck on the cheek. And he lost his fucken mind after that.'

'Elite? Jesus. He's hardly a work of art, is he? I mean, yeah, he's got the height, but the bloke had a healthy pair of tits last time I looked.'

'Yeah, well, I think he realised that after that. Turned all feral and started hanging out at all these scungy backpacker bars on Queen Street. Those fire hazard ones, deep down in basements. That's where he met his first girlfriend. She was from Japan. English language student. He sponsored her for a visa, but she shot through soon after the paperwork got stamped to check out Uluru or Great Barrier Reef or some shit like that. Then, a few months later, he met his next one. She was American this time, working as an au pair in Toorak. He sponsored her for a visa too. Even managed to convince this one to move in with him. Then six months later she went back to Bumfuck Idaho for her ten-year high school reunion and left the dancehall with Johnny Football Hero. Phoned it in to Bones from the middle of a cornfield, moments before Johnny ploughed her in the back of his pickup. So, strictly speaking, not cheating.'

'Right, that's all my clothes, then,' I say. 'Go chuck this bag with the others by the front door, and I'll grab the PlayStation.'

I head into the living room, and I get down on my hands and knees and reach around to unhook the cable from the back of the television. Max helps himself to a seat on the black leather couch in the living room and chucks his feet up on the polished oak coffee table. The cunt's making himself quite at home, he is. Starts flicking through the coffee-table book too. One of hers, on the early works of Picasso.

'Then what happened?' I ask.

'Well, yeah, this is where it all gets a bit messed up. Bones ended up falling in love. Fell hard too. It's the Belarus one, this time. Met her at Club 33 of all places. Fuck knows what she was doing hanging out at that fucken hovel. Honestly though, to Bones's credit, she was an absolute stunner. Had that

Eastern European model look. Trained lawyer too, doing some postgrad stuff at Melbourne Uni. That was her excuse for being in the country anyway. Bones got all righteous about it, though. Harping on about it all the time. Telling us that there's someone for everyone and when you know, you know. All that shit.'

'Surprised Trent didn't take a swing at him for that.'

'Came close to blows a couple of times. Really close. Anyway, Bones knocks this new one up and proposes. A month later, he's back at immigration signing up for round three. Just a couple of standard forms to fill in so fiancé and foetus can stay in the country. Or so he thought. He walks up to the counter, and the clerk behind the desk goes, "Get fucked, mate. Already played your two jokers." Turns out you can only sponsor two chicks in Australia before the Crown cuts off your tab.'

I go to the hallway closet and reach up to the top shelf and take down the air mattress, my sleeping bag, and a spare pillow. I notice a black and white polka dot umbrella leaning up against the back corner. It holds my eye, until Max breaks my train of thought.

'So, one month later, Bones is dragging three large suitcases and a pregnant missus up twenty flights of stairs to her parent's apartment, in the middle of a Belarus blizzard. No other option. Started taking Slavic language lessons to try to reignite his real estate career. Ended up getting marched less than a week into the job. Got a gig cleaning train carriages instead. Graveyard shift. They were still living with her parents too. All three generations, all under the one roof.'

'Jesus Christ. I'm almost starting to feel sorry for the cunt.'

Though in truth, pairing Bones's current lot alongside my

own is somewhat soothing.

'Last I heard from him,' Max goes on, 'was a postcard he sent me. He was on holiday with the in-laws at some swamp thing that claimed itself to be a lake. It was so depressing that I chucked it straight in the bin. Two years ago, that was. Last I heard from him.'

'That's me done,' I say. 'I'll just grab my toothbrush, and we're good to go.'

'Anyway, it all goes to prove my point that I've been saying for years. Ask a girl where she's from, and the town she tells you will be your tomb.'

I wander into the bathroom and over to the marble vanity. From the porcelain jar with the pink sea shell on it, I pluck my blue toothbrush that rests beside her pink one. I turn to leave. The door to the toilet is ajar. And I see it. I fucken see it, alright. My shoulders tense and a rage fires from deep within. The fucken toilet seat is up.

Chapter 11
Paradoxical Undressing

Ed's smiling at me. I'm at my desk, it's Thursday, and I'm trying to catch up on all the work I missed while I was at Ed's funeral. That was yesterday, that was. I've kept the funeral program on my desk for show. Though, Ed's big grinning face staring at me while I'm trying to work is becoming somewhat distracting. It's a photograph of him on the back of a boat, holding up a snapper at a deceptive angle that—of course—makes the fish look bigger and his nose look smaller. I'll bin it by close of business today. Also, for all of Ed's claims, his funeral was a massive cock fest which all but confirms my theory on him. I should tell William of Ockham to strop another fucken razor. Old Rick put in a courtesy call to the cops Monday morning. The security cameras said the bouncer was acting in self-defence, and the chalk marks said the working mum wasn't speeding gratuitously, just a touch overeager to get her kid home from the commercial orphanage the poor bastard had spent the preceding fourteen hours at. Case closed. Though, I'm doubtful it was ever opened.

My boss was off crook Monday and Tuesday. Showed up late to Ed's funeral yesterday. Sat at the back. Still looked rough. The church was fucken freezing, those old oil heaters were doing fuck all for the cold, but my boss was still mopping sweat off his forehead with his handkerchief. This morning, he walked into work with a nod, a smile, and a shiny new gym bag. The door to his office has been closed almost ever since. The only time I've seen him other than when he first arrived, was when he fixed himself a shake of some sachet shit in the kitchen around lunchtime.

'I've found out some more about Friday,' Will says. 'It's actually really interesting.'

He's been going on and on about this ad nauseam since Monday morning, and it's doing my fucken head in now. The Mayor of Melbourne should implement a debarking program for these loud mouth office extraverts, as far as I'm concerned.

'Will, mate. I'm busy dealing with the utter mess of Ed's handovers, on top of all my own shit,' I say. 'You can help me out if you don't have enough to do.'

'Wait, wait. Listen to this, listen,' he says, scrolling his mouse. 'Looks like the same thing happened in Russia in 1959. This group of friends went for a quiet camp in the snow, and they all died naked.'

Will's claiming his impromptu nudie run last Friday night was the result of a psychological phenomenon called paradoxical undressing. From what I've half heard from his across-desk spiel, when the body experiences shock, signals get mixed up. Will reckons his brain told him he was hot, when he was cold.

'That's fucken fantastic, Will,' I say. 'Thank you very much for that, I am enlightened.'

Tell you what, open plan offices will be the death of someone one day. If this barrage of words were being made by any tongue other than Will's, there'd be blood spilt on keyboards, that's for fair fucken certain.

'Jackson, have you located that Parker invoice yet?' Rick calls from his desk, his hand covering the mouthpiece of his phone. 'I've got Sydney on the line.'

'Fuck. Hadn't had a chance to look yet, mate. Warner keeps spewing at me about his new premiums, so I'm trying to flush this shit first.'

When I'm team leader, I'll be the one asking the fucken questions, and the first thing I'll do is delegate this account to Rick. Warner's worth about thirty million from bouncing between companies as CEO, collecting golden hand jobs on the way. But still the cunt goes through his life policy, clause by subclause. You can't get any sort of amendment past Warner without him completely losing his shit. His latest message brings an abrupt end to our back and forth exchange of the last two hours.

'Enough, Jackson. I'm stopping by your office at 4 P.M. I expect to have my requests actioned upon my arrival. W.'

I haven't told Rick or Will or my boss about what went down Friday. Never hand a bloke free ammunition. I'll slowly drop hints over the next fortnight that I'm getting bored of my relationship, and then I'll eventually tell them that I was the one who called it off. I'll tell them that she kicked me out onto the street all angry, crying, and she threw my clothes over the balcony, and I threw my keys back up at her, and I yelled out to her from the street that I was sorry, that I can't help what I feel, and that it was just something I felt in my gut. And I'll tell them I've crashed at a mate's place for a bit, until I find a nice place of my own.

Chapter 12

Fentanyl

A client face-to-face meeting. Warner is yelling at me, a silver fox with mange. His skin clings to his face, dry from the winter air, as if it could collapse at any time in an avalanche of old dead man skin, leaving only his bloody skull and angry eyes to stare death at me. We're in our only meeting room, next to my boss's office, although the cheapest-quote glass allows everyone to hear every word of every conversation. It's a small space with only a small round table to separate us, and a large fluorescent light that burn my eyes.

It's obvious that Warner got the shit kicked out of him in high school and his entire career has been built around trying to inverse this schoolyard hierarchy. The bloke could retire tomorrow if he chose to do so. Several passive-income streams. A permanent mooring in Bora Bora; afternoons chasing mahi-mahi by sunset. He could have what the rest of this world wants right now—to be on holiday all the time, but instead, he's spent the last thirty minutes unleashing his unresolved rage at me. The conversation continues to go around in circles, until he finally threatens to escalate matters with management.

'I'll do it if I have to, Jackson. Watch me fucken do it, cunt.'

'You're more than welcome to speak with Carl, but he'll tell you the same.'

'You think I'm fucken stupid, Jackson? You think I'm fucken weak?'

'No. But, as I've reiterated many times during the last week, recent incidents identified by your life insurance provider has caused them to reassess your risk level.'

(i) Stupid

(ii) Sick

(iii) Fuck

Warner overdosed in a hotel room out by the airport last Christmas Eve. Fentanyl. The hooker phoned an ambulance, and the hospital notified the police. Somewhere along the line, his life insurance provider found out, and they sent me a message last month to tell me they were jacking up his premiums. Wife, four kids, three under five; all none the wiser. When I informed Warner of this slight readjustment to his outgoings in account of his self-inflicted medical misadventure, he immediately interpreted it as some sort of schoolyard beat up, and we've been in a fierce message exchange ever since. One that's inevitably found its way to face-to-face form.

'I couldn't have been fucken clearer, Jackson. Switch providers. Negotiate a better deal. That's your fucken job,' he says.

'I tried my best, but—'

'You *can* read, can't you? Because I'm confused by your confusion.'

'No one wanted to touch your policy. They all talk between themselves. All of them.'

'And how hard did you try, Jackson? Some life advice on the house. Passivity is a repellent. Once someone smells it on you, you're fucken done.'

And I jump the desk. I grab the lapels of Warner's suit jacket and throw him as hard as I can off his chair. I pin him on the ground and use his lapels to lift his face towards mine.

'You think your walls are real, Warner?'

His tan oxford shoes kick at the air, but I can feel he's weak. I whisper in his ear, 'Still in school, cunt.'

Rick runs in, followed by my boss, and they both try to pull me off him, but I only let go when Will joins in too.

****

I'm sitting in my boss's office. He's closed the blinds so that Rick and Will can't see in, but you can be sure as hell their ears will be up against the glass. Warner left in a hurry as soon as he got to his feet. They always do those types.

'I can't tolerate violence in the workplace, Jackson,' my boss says from behind his desk. 'Especially against clients.'

'It was because he was at me.'

My boss nods.

'Some parts of my younger self, I see in you, Jackson.'

Fuck no.

'How long have you been with us?' he asks.

'It'll be seven years in November.'

'Seven years. That's a decent innings. And you're great at your job. I must give credit where credit is due. The issue is this, though: Sydney will somehow find out about this. They always do. And then they'll come to me asking questions. And they'll want to know what I did about it.'

He gets up and starts doing stretches behind his desk. He does a few neck rolls, looks up at the ceiling, and arches his back.

'But I know why you're angry, Jackson. You're an easy book to read.'

He sits back down in his chair and leans forward across the desk with his fingers interlocked.

'It's the whole Ed thing, isn't it?'

And I nod.

'Look,' he says, 'the only ace left up my sleeve, is this.'

He leans down to his side and thumbs about in his top drawer. He slides a card across the desk.

'The Shrink'

'She does *Late Night Fridays*,' he says. 'Give her a call and see if she can tee up a time for you tomorrow. Then my arse is covered, and your arse is saved.'

'Thanks, Carl. I appreciate it. What about Warner?'

'Don't worry about that fucken arsehole. He owes me a couple of favours anyway.'

I get up to leave but stop at the door. I walk back towards my boss.

'Oh, before I forget,' I say, taking out my wallet. 'You dropped this Friday night.'

I slide the corporate credit card across his desk. His eyes take a quick glance at the card, but they refuse to meet mine. He moves his mouse around a little bit and stares at his computer screen, feigning work.

'Close the door behind you, Jackson.'

Chapter 13

Session One

There's a massive diamond on her ring finger. That's the first thing I notice. Excessive in size, as far as I'm concerned. I'm sitting on a red chair. It's comfy to be fair. Nice soft arm rests. She's sitting across from me on another red chair, same as mine. When I get a place of my own, I'm going to buy a chair just like this one and sit in it all day and try my best to think of fuck all.

This room has polished concrete floors, white walls, with three tall windows that look out at the arse end of a brick building across the laneway, one floor above street level. Between our red chairs, lies a low coffee table that houses a small cactus collection.

I'd pick her as late-fifties or perhaps a sixty who's taken care of herself. Red heels, grey skirt, black thick-rimmed glasses, and hair tied up in a bun to complete the cliché. She's already scribbling in her little notepad. It's hot in here. Sweat sticks my shirt to my back, and my eyes feel dry under the artificial light.

'Not too cold for you in here?' she asks. 'I can turn up the heater if you'd like?'

'No, I'm fine, thanks,' I say.

'Do you prefer Jack or Jackson?'

'Jackson.'

'Tell me about your relationship with your father, Jackson.'

'He's dead. Died when I was younger. Slipped. Hit his head on the bathroom floor.'

'How old were you when that happened?

'Six.'

'Who found him?'

'Our cleaner.'

'Any siblings?' she says, her pen scribbling furiously.

'No.'

'And your mother?'

'What about her?'

'How is your relationship with her?'

'She lives in Tasmania. Married some poppy farmer she met at a dark arts festival.'

'Do you see her much?'

'Who?'

'Your mother.'

'I visited her the Christmas before last. It was an epileptic fit that killed my dad. That's why he slipped.'

'Does she visit you? Your mother?'

'I don't think she cares for Melbourne anymore.'

'Do you have a wife, or a girlfriend, or a partner?'

'Yes.'

'Which one?'

'A girlfriend.'

'How long have you been with her for?'

'Six years.'

'And it's a stable relationship?'

'Yes.'

'Have you ever harmed yourself?'

'No.'

'Her?'

'No.'

'Has she every harmed you?'

'No.'

'You were referred here by your employer. Your boss briefed me on an incident at your work. I was also informed of the tragic event last Friday. That must have been a traumatic experience.'

'Yes.'

'How did it make you feel?'

I shrug.

'Have you been experiencing feelings of anger?' she asks.

'No.'

'Are you so sure, Jackson?'

'These things can happen to anyone, can't they?'

'You lashed out physically at a client. It could be argued that this was a physical manifestation of suppressed anger.'

'No. It was because he was at me.'

'Would you describe your action as out of character?'

'Yes.'

'Conflict is unavoidable. Violence, not so. How have you dealt with conflict in your past?'

'I haven't had to deal with it too often.'

'Have you ever fought with your girlfriend?'

'Never.'

'Not once?'

'Hardly ever, really.'

'Did you fight with your father?'

'Never.'

'Your mother?'

'Only after.'

'What did you fight about?'

'I don't know. Stupid stuff, mostly. Christmas trees. Stuff like that.'

'Did you have anger towards her?'

'Some.'

'About what, exactly?'

'I don't know. Just about everything really.'

'Jackson, sometimes even when no one is at fault, we still search out someone to blame.'

'This wasn't like that.'

'Our time is up, Jackson. We'll pick it up from here next Friday.'

Chapter 14

Trent Stench

The lights at Copper Room are a moody orange. The ceiling low and littered with assorted chandeliers. The lounge area, where I'm sitting, is filled with vintage chairs and tables and couches, that are in turn filled with poets, hustlers, and entrepreneurs. I wish I had another choice other than this. But the horrific alternative of spending my Saturday night on that shitty sofa in the sole company of Max has left me no other option. Max said he was too poor to come out. Spent too much money fixing the hot water heater last month. Some bullshit like that.

I'm sitting by myself at a table for two, with only my Negroni for company. I'm sitting alone like some sort of creep because—of course—he's intentionally late. I even arrived a half hour behind time myself, anticipating this move, but the arsehole's gone the full hour himself. I should have expected that. His way of wrestling back control after I insisted on starting at Copper Room, mainly because I know he'll hate this place. Can't give this cunt one inch of advantage. You always need to start Trent on the back foot. Absolute nightmare otherwise. The only reason society evolved to its current state is to control people like Trent. If it wasn't for his ability to conceptualise consequence in the form of a custodial sentence, Trent would be nothing more than a chimpanzee tearing off your face. Like that one that had a go at Nigel Lassiter that time when they brought it into studio to perform sign language. That's Trent. A fucken psychopathic pet chimpanzee.

****

'Well, this place is fucken dead,' Trent says as he finally rocks up. In actuality, there are forty or so others at Copper Room. By 'dead' Trent's referencing the lack of unaccompanied single girls between the ages of eighteen and twenty-five smashing Chartreuse shots at the bar. Trent is all sharp angles. Always has been. Sharp nose, sharp chin, a decent head of hair combed to sharp side part. Trent's head hates a curve so much he's got no earlobes. Max pointed it out once, and now it's all I see. Trent's lobeless ears. He hasn't aged as bad as Max, but I'm still rather shocked at how deep his frown lines are as he screws up his forehead.

'Trust you to choose a shithole like this, Jackson,' he says. 'All fucken couples. C'mon, let's find another bar.'

Because in Trent's mind, one block over and one block up, some bloke is about to poleaxe his soulmate out the back of a bar, next to the empty kegs, in some sadistic sliding door scenario that's currently playing out in his head.

'Chill, man,' I say. 'A girl from work said she might be coming here with friends. Get a drink, take a seat. It's still early, we've got the rest of the night to bounce about.'

'Alright, fine,' he says, with the prospect of potential female companionship acting as mental ointment for the time being.

Trent returns with a beer and takes his seat, his head

jagging around as he surveys the bar in every direction. He's squirming in his chair at the lack of opportunity the Copper Room clientele presents.

'What's the name of this girl from work?' Trent asks.

'Melanie. How's things with you? Still fixing computers?'

'Well, it's more than that. Data security for major phone companies. She single, this Melanie?'

'Pay well?'

'Not really. Not what you'd think. Not what it fucken should anyway. So, Max tells me you've moved in with him.'

'Just for a bit. Till I find a nice place of my own.'

'What are you going to do? Rent or buy?'

'Not sure yet,' I say.

'Well, don't be a fuckin idiot and do what Max did.'

'What? Buy a house?'

'Yes. That.'

'Bad investment, you reckon?'

'Bad decision all round. You reckon that mildew ridden, rotting cesspit is worth anywhere close to what Max paid for it? No fucken way. A mortgage is nothing more than an emotionally inflated stay of eviction. It's all a fucken hysteria, in my book.'

'Still, I don't know. Gives him some sense of security, though, doesn't it?'

'No, it fucken doesn't, Jackson. It's punching in a dream. That's all that shit is. Plenty of blokes with their mortgage paid off in full, jump in front of trains every other fucken day in this town.'

'Well, we can compare notes in fifty-years' time, then, when Max is getting his arse wiped for him with fancy four-ply, and we're scraping ours ourselves with pages torn from last week's Best Bets.'

'Yeah, well I don't plan to be around long enough to see that anyway. Gonna let nature take its course. Anyway, I'm dying for a smoke. C'mon, let's check out the beer garden.'

'Jesus Christ. Really? It'll be fucken freezing outside.'

'Yeah, but there might be some chicks out there to talk to. You never know. Beats sitting here shooting shit between ourselves.'

****

It's not raining, it hasn't done all day, but the entire back courtyard is inexplicably wet. A moss-covered stone wall, dug into the steep gradient of the rising street, is dripping some sort of fluorescent yellow discharge into a blocked drain filled with green sludge. There's a vandalised outhouse with a wooden door hanging off its hinges, out-housing a stainless-steel toilet with no toilet seat. All the cobblestones move underfoot. There's a rusty old heat lamp in the centre of the courtyard, yet to be turned on. No one else is outside, bar us and a moth that keeps bouncing off the cracked orange light above.

'When did you start smoking?' I ask Trent.

'Bout a year back. Conversation starter. "Wanna light?", "Gotta light?" Depending on what the circumstance calls for.'

He points his pack in my direction.

'Nah, I'm all good. Cheers.'

'Good. These things cost a fucken fortune these days,' he says. 'So, you get up to much last night?'

'Nah, crashed out early.'

'Fuck me, Jackson. They don't reimburse you for unused Fridays on your death bed, you know?'

'Woke up fresh, though. Plenty in the tank for tonight.'

'I'll give you that. The only two parts of life I can tolerate are drunk Friday nights and fresh Saturday mornings. They're quite at odds with each other, though. See, the main issue I have with these blowout Saturdays is they're haunted all night by Monday morning. But fuck it, I'll do it if I have to, given the hellish alternative. So, here I am.'

'What did you do last night, then?'

'Was far from fresh when I woke up this morning, that's for certain.'

'Yeah? Big one?'

'Went on one of those organised bar crawls. Twenty bucks a ticket. Gets you free entry to all the bars and a free wet pussy at the first one.'

'Who'd you go with?'

'The others on the bar crawl.'

'Who?'

'People new to Melbourne.'

'What? Students and backpackers?'

'People. New to Melbourne. What? You wanna hear all their fucken backstories, do ya?'

'How'd you go, then?'

'So-so. Somehow managed to lose everyone at the end of the night, though. This Melanie chick that's coming. You after her or what?'

'Might be coming. And no. Office too small for that. Don't shit where you eat and all that. But yes, as far as I'm aware, she's single. So please, be my guest. I reckon you two might get along.'

'Okay, good to know. Good, good,' Trent takes a drag of his cigarette and exhales out the corner of his mouth. 'Anyway, Jackson, don't for a second think this home ownership mess

Max got himself into was a result of some hot coals motivational shit. Truth is, this time last year, Max was partying like a fucken maniac. He was living in some shed at the back of some squalor share house, out Northcote way. Nearly as bad as his pad now. Anyway, the caretaker from his school lent him this dating bible to read one lunchtime. Messed up his head big time. He became obsessed with the pursuit. Going out every night; rain, hail, or shine. Nights were for partying, work was for hangovers. And he's a fucken primary school teacher, remember. Try to get your head around that hell. Kids clawing at the classroom windows each morning trying to escape the stench of Max's beer sweats.'

There's a strong wind in the courtyard. It's collecting between the skyscrapers, becoming colder and colder as it swirls down towards us and burrows into our skin. I walk over to the heat lamp and try to get it working. The starter clicks, but it seems to be out of gas. There's a slight moment of respite from the wind, but then a heavy gust rolls through, and we both hunch in silence as the wind dances between us, until it passes.

'Anyway,' Trent goes on, 'the only night Max wouldn't go out was Monday. Every Monday he went back to Albert Park for a roast dinner with the folks. So, the only time his parents ever saw him would be on the tail end of a massive six-day bender. As you can imagine, it's not a pretty sight. No chat, bloated, sweaty face rashes. Just sitting there mute, pushing potatoes around his plate. And so, his parents became slightly concerned for his mental state. Now, he was okay, as far as I know, but as I said, the only time *they* saw him was when he was very, very, very hungover. Which, to be fair to them, is almost indistinguishable from someone suffering from chronic clinical depression. So, one Monday night, right after ice cream, they sit him down all serious. Said they were worried about him, worried about what he was doing with his life. They wanted to help him out, help him grow up, help him become a man. A *man*, Jackson! So, they presented him an opportunity. Max's folks had found that shithole in Coburg and then kissed him on the dick with a house deposit. He moved in a month later, with a forty-year mortgage to cuddle up to at night.'

'And that's that, then,' I say. 'One more cunt swallowed by the suburbs.'

'Victim of circumstance more than anything. Funny thing is, though, Max had this initial hope that this home ownership thing would help him in his pursuit of company. He went out on a date soon after he moved in. Dropped it into the conversation, straight off the bat. Boom! "I own a house." Didn't even register on her radar. The girl was just disgusted he'd never been to the Amalfi Coast. He never heard from her again.'

'I went there a couple of years back, the Amalfi Coast.'

'Anyway, Max stayed home a lot after that. Hardly ever comes out now. Shit state-of-affairs he's got himself into. Goes to prove all those A's he got back at school, count for fuck all out here in the real world. How often did I tell him that that would be the case?'

'A lot,' I say, pulling my phone from my pocket.

'Yes. A fucken prophet, I am. Right all along.'

'Ah, shit,' I say, staring at my phone.

'What? What?'

I sigh and shake my head.

'What, man?' Trent asks.

'Melanie just messaged me. Says she's not heading into the city anymore. She's having a quiet night in now.'

And judging by the expression on his face, if it wasn't for the laws imposed on us by Buckingham Palace, Trent would be ripping off my face right now.

Chapter 15

Leer, Reek, Less

The music inside Melbourne Town Hall is too loud for us to talk. That's why we're hanging out in the foyer area between the coat check and the shitters. It's also cos this seems to be where all the girls are too. After copping a vicious spray from Trent over my complete inability to run a decent night, I surrendered to his idea of going to this EDM gig, content in knowing his cage had been sufficiently rattled to my satisfaction. He assured me, placing both hands on my shoulders, that this place would be 'full of hot chicks.' And while the ticket price stung on entry, to be fair to Trent, the ratio here is unreal. Everywhere I look, I see girls dressed to the nines. Clusters of three or four or five, traverse the red carpeted floor of the foyer, sipping straws from long glasses stuffed with lemons and limes and mint leaves. Never in one spot for too long. Always looking like they've lost a friend and are trying to work out where she got to.

'So, you actually like this music?' I ask Trent.

'Yeah, big into it.'

'I just feel a lot of this stuff is *Emperor's Clothes* shit sometimes.'

'Nah, this dude's legit. My brother got me into his stuff ages ago.'

'The one from your dad's first marriage?'

'Yeah, that one.'

'What's he up to these days?'

'My dad or my brother?'

'Your brother.'

'No idea,' Trent says, picking at the label of his beer. 'Surfing or something.'

'Anyway, all I'm saying is you can hardly sing along to this sort of music, can you? Just some DJ's dick ticket, as far as I'm concerned.'

****

We're a few more rounds in now, still parked up in the corner of the foyer, and as if six years had never passed, Trent's dishing out his avant-garde girl advice.

'It's like this, Jackson. Chicks, whether they admit to it or not, always impress an aesthetic hierarchy onto their group of friends. This is different to guys. Both of us are standing here firmly believing that we're the better looking one of the two.'

I'm far better looking than Picasso face right here, that is for fair fucken certain.

'But girls, Jackson. They know exactly their place in rank within their group. It is an unspoken but definitive truth. So, I'll keep this simple for you. Three girls are sitting at a bar. Gold, Silver, and Bronze. Now, most guys would most likely hit on Silver. That being their intuitive compromise between their ego and their self-consciousness. But let's say Silver stiff arms him. This leaves him with only one girl at the bar that he has any chance with: Bronze. Because the hierarchical law these girls abide by, unequivocally states, a man can only work his way *down* the order. Now, what if he was to go straight for

Gold from the get go? Sure, she might shut him down. More likely than not. But Silver and Bronze saw him go up to Gold. Now, that is a man who goes after what he wants, that is a man with confidence, and most important of all, that is a man who has two more lives remaining: Silver and Bronze. That's why you should always go for Gold, Jackson.' Trent slaps me on the arm. 'You might even get lucky once-in-a-while. Stand at the top of the podium, hand on heart, as they play Advance Australia Fair in your honour.'

I fucken hate it when Trent touches me, even in play, and part of me wants to knock his fucken jaw off his skull right now. I let it slide this time, though. Truly an exercise in self-control, hanging out with this cunt.

'Alright, ya fucken savant,' I say. 'Let's get in there and see how your theory plays out in real life. Didn't drop three pineapples at the door to stand in a fucken foyer all night.'

****

The undercard is onstage: some petite girl with dreadlocks and oversized headphones. She's leaning over her decks, wanting fuck all to do with the crowd. Bass is dropped. The main act, Trent told me earlier, is some Scottish DJ who was big in the nineties and who now seems to be enjoying some sort of renaissance based on a crowd that looks to have been born well after his initial success, bar the scattering of Charlie Chaplins leering at all the girls from the shadowy fringes of the dancefloor.

Our drinks go down quicker, our pisses more frequent, and the only conversations between Trent and myself are yelling in each other's ear, 'I'm going to the bar,' or, 'I'm going for a piss.' And I'm still nowhere near drunk enough to dance. Not even fucken close. Girls stand nearby, and I smile at them, but the most I get back is an obligatory return smile, and when I return their return smile with a tiny little wave, it's met with a look of utter contempt, and they turn away in disgust. Fucken hell. I know I'm going to need to dance, so I down my beer and tell Trent, 'I'm going to the bar.'

I down a double shot of absinthe to kick things along and return to Trent with a couple of fresh beers. I nod my head in time to the music, willing my body to relax and to feel the rhythm. I start to softly punch my bottle to the beat. Trent's swaying on the spot. If one didn't know better, you might mistake it as interpretive dance, but I know Trent is void of any sense of artistry and what I am seeing next to me is purely an impairment of motor function. Those clusters of girls we saw earlier have inexplicably vanished, and groups of blokes a dozen strong torrent onto the dancefloor. Broad shoulders in bursting V-neck fitted T's fill every conceivable gap there once was with a reek of body odour as vile as I've smelt since Bones's flabby smegma tits brushed past me in the boys changing rooms at Albert Park Grammar. The room has been napalmed by cock. I turn to Trent to ask him what the fuck this is all about, but he's gone.

****

I've been standing by myself for some time, my beer long gone due to the pace of my solitary drinking. The DJ, the bigshot Scottish one, takes to the stage. The crowd cheers, hands up in the air, unleashing a blitzkrieg of armpit stench. He's balding, the DJ is. The last of his sandy hair barely clinging to the edges of his head. He's wearing a poorly filled crew-neck T of all sorts of colours, a slipping psychedelic grip on a youth long passed. The noise starts.

RWAH

RWAH

RWAH, RWAH, RWAH

RWAH

RWAH

RWAH, RWAH, RWAH

The giant speaker stacks hanging on each side of the stage fire air pulses into the crowd. Shoulders clip me on the swarm to the front of the stage. Everyone starts dancing with themselves. My head hangs heavy, and the beer in my stomach rises towards the top of my throat to tell me, 'You're fucken done, mate. More than fucken done.' Everyone here is a cunt.

> You're only here
> Because of her

Trent's not coming back, and in a crowd of a thousand or two, I stand alone.

Chapter 16

Wolf Creep

It's Monday afternoon, and I'm still feeling the burn from Saturday night. I'm at my desk, and my brain, eyes, and throat are as dry as the kitty shit that Max kicked into the corner of the hallway in lieu of forken out for a fucken vacuum cleaner. I couldn't even find a brush and shovel anywhere in the house, so I had to pick up the shit with some toilet paper and chuck it out the front door into the raging weeds and thorns and vines that make up Max's front yard. My hand is shaking on my mouse as I scroll down the latest garbage message sent to me by my boss. I give it a half glance on the off chance it holds some relevance to my job or, as a fucken long shot, my life.

It doesn't.

Delete.

When people talk about hangovers, they typically talk of the physical first. Hot flushes, sweats, headaches, nausea, shakes, all that usual trite. But they are the least of your worries. The very least. The most painful part of a hangover is that when you wake up hung, it's the most realistic snapshot of your life possible. Your hopes and dreams stay passed out on the bathroom floor long after you drag yourself to work

Monday morning. All you have until they find you again is what you have in the moment. An air mattress, a pillow, a sleeping bag, a toothbrush, a PlayStation, and the corner of a beaten lime sofa. It's you, as clear as day, honest in the moment, too sick to dream, too ill to fake yourself. That's what hurts most about being hungover. It's always the truth that hurts the most.

****

My boss has a girl in his office, around Will's age. This has been going on all day. Earlier this morning, my boss muttered something under his breath about rectifying the company's gender imbalance as he paced nervously around the office, sucking in his guts before the first interviewee arrived. But I know exactly what is going on here. A creep in feminist clothing. The applicant in his office leaves as another arrives. She's taller than him, this one. A shake of her hand, a peck on the cheek. If his hand didn't rub the small of her back as he ushered her into his office, it came fucken close to it. He winks at us as he shuts the door behind them.

'Disgusting,' I say, shaking my head.

'Cut him some slack, Jackson,' Rick says.

'All I'm saying, is he's fucken hallucinating if he thinks he has a chance with any of that lot.'

My boss is interviewing today for Ed's replacement, which has delayed his decision on the team leader position. All things being even, I'd consider this a sizeable setback, but the one benefit of this particular scenario is that it allows some time for my Warner indiscretion to fade from recent memory.

'Yeah, well, he's had a hard time of it of late,' Rick says, his white cactus hair buried in his keyboard. 'And anyway, the office could do with a bit more of a balance.'

'Yes, it certainly fucken could,' I say. 'But you know, and I know, this is not what *that's* about,' and I point hard at the closed door of my boss's office.

'Maybe it's cos they're cheaper?' Will says.

'Can't say that, mate,' Rick says.

'What? Graduates?' Will asks.

I drag my hand down my hot bloated face, 'Will, please.'

'Anyway, Jackson,' Rick says, his shaving rash chin rising from his keyboard, 'after your Warner meltdown last week, I hardly think you're one to pass judgement on office morality.'

The only regret I have of that incident now is this pink-skinned, white-haired wanker now feels entitled to pass judgement.

'That was different,' I say.

'Well, from where I'm sitting, you owe a lot to Carl. He didn't have to give you a second chance. Stuck his neck out to Sydney to save your arse.'

'Warner made his bed. The cunt can take his temazepam and sleep in it, as far as I'm concerned. I don't care how entitled or elitist these fucks think they are, they can watch their fucken tongue when they talk to me.'

****

Girls continue to come and go. My boss is fully embracing the concept of diversity in the workplace. All shades of lipstick high heel their way into his office. To be fair, though, I do need to settle myself down. I owe my boss fuck all, but the Warner incident was a little too close for comfort. Life's an icy slope, and every-now-and-then you need to chuck the ice axe into the side of the mountain. Keep it together, steady the ship.

Take stock, rebuild. Find a new girl before any of these sad sacks-of-shit realise the last one's gone.

'Rick, how old were you when you had your first kid?' I ask him.

He leans back in his chair, his white eyebrows arching at the fact that I've asked him about himself for the first time in nearly seven years.

'I was forty-nine when Brayden came along. Bit of a late start. Took a brave woman to reign this terror in. And it's not like the first load stuck in her right away. Couple of false—'

'So, last night, the missus gave me the clock-ticking speech,' I say. 'Told me that six years was long enough to wait.'

'She did, did she? You gotta expect that chat to happen sooner or later, mate.'

'I told her straight up that I'm not ready. Not right now anyway. Turned into a bit of a blue. Ended up crashing at a mate's place.'

'Trouble in paradise, huh?'

Fucken lippy cunt.

'Tell her to freeze her eggs,' Will says.

'Thanks, mate,' I say. 'I'll clear out some space in the freezer tonight. Throw out a bag of freezer-burnt peas to make way. Fuck me, your advice sometimes.'

And then I see her. She walks through the frosted doors with the company logo. Jet black hair and piercing blue eyes that never break from a smile.

'Right place?' she asks me, without saying a word.

I reply with a nod.

Sometimes, when you know, you know. And I know she's got the job.

Chapter 17

Session Two

Friday night. We're both sitting in our red chairs, and once again she's started scribbling in her little notepad without me saying one fucken word. She's had a haircut since last week. The bun's been lobbed off. The suburban stylist has made a complete and utter mess of it, though. Really hacked into it bad.

'Do you think they took too much off?' she would have asked her husband as she pinched her mutilated bangs in the mirror.

'No, not at all,' he would have replied. 'I mean to say—It'll grow back anyway, won't it?'

And she would have turned and stared death at him and stormed upstairs and slammed the door to their master bedroom as hard as she could. Poor cunt. No waking up from that fucken nightmare.

'Have you heard that time heals all wounds, Jackson?'

'Yes.'

'It'll just take some time, they say. It doesn't. Time heals nothing, not by a long way. Pain and suffering must be cleaned, excised, before it has a chance to heal. Otherwise, in time, it will suffocate your heart, fuse your bones, and burrow its way deep into your mind and marrow. Left untreated, it can make you do things you never believed you could. Are you following?'

'Yes.'

'It will fester, stew, consume you. Thoughts, simple basic thoughts, will grow. They'll become bigger, bigger ideas, and they'll unravel, unfold upon themselves. You will question which world is truer. The one outside your eyes or the one inside your head. And once you release your rage at the world, you can never go back to how it was. You will kill who you once were. Are you following?'

'Yes.'

'What is the answer, though, Jackson? What is the answer to your pain? How can you find peace? Closure, Jackson. Closure. You can't bury it. You need to incinerate it. Consider it a tumour. You need to open the wound, tear at the flesh housing your pain, find every poisoned part, and cut it all away. Decimate the tendrils wrapped around your being. Piece by piece, until no trace is left. Know your sickness, know yourself. It's one and the same. Vengeance sung, is both violence and art. They are two poles of the same problem. But let me be clear: You must never let violence escape yourself. You are its watch. Do you understand what I'm saying?'

'Yes.'

'Men don't bear children, Jackson. A man's only connection to immortality is his name, and he rips it from deep within himself and places it in the arms of the world, bruised and bloodied and screaming for help. Does this make any sense to you?'

'Yes.'

'Never mistake time for an antiseptic. Your soul does not

care for time and space. Closure is what it hungers for. Find it. Only then can you rest peacefully.'

'Okay.'

'Our time is up. We'll pick it up from here next Friday.'

Chapter 18

Dear Max

Saturday night. I'm walking with Max down a long, lowly lit corridor to Trent's thirty-fourth floor apartment carrying a slab of beer. It's right amongst all the chaos of the CBD, a couple of blocks down from Victoria Market. It's one of those massive modern skyscrapers made of all mirror glass, with no balconies, and surrounded in every direction by the skeletons of next year's editions, cranes on rooves, who will soon dwarf this one and cast it forever in eternal shadow.

Max reckons half the occupants of Trent's apartment tower are network marketing their vaginas by the hour, which means Trent's essentially paying through his scalene nose to live in a brothel. In the foyer, in front of the ten or so lifts, there were at least half-a-dozen grimy loose cuts looking lost, trying to work out how the fuck to get up to whatever floor they were told to come up to. I wouldn't be surprised if Trent has worked out a mate's rates deal with a neighbour down the hall, for whenever his dry gets too much for his mind.

Max bangs hard on Trent's door. A few numbers along, some old, obese fuck wearing a beige crew-neck T, loose cuts, and white tennis shoes, creeps out into the corridor. A door slams quickly shut behind him. He nods to us as he passes, trailing with him a waft of rancid sweat.

Max didn't want to come out tonight. Said he's never felt a strong need to celebrate his birthday. Just another day in his book. I insisted. Told him to shit and shower, cos fuck let another Saturday night go by sitting alone on his smelly fucken sofa. Trent was an easier sell, as expected. Told him we'd stop by his place and head out into the city from there. Sneak in a couple of cheap ones first. Pays to watch the coin from time to time in this town. And with Trent it makes three, so these two useless fucks can keep each other company while I try to get this life shit back on track.

I did it once.

I can do it again.

Trent opens the door topless, sporting a skinny-fat frame.

'Took your fucken time,' he says.

'There was an obstruction on the tracks,' I say.

I chuck the slab on his kitchenette counter, rip open the cardboard housing, and disperse the first round. The necks of our three bottles collide.

'Cheers, boys,' I say.

'Happy Birthday, Max,' Trent says. 'Jesus Christ. Thirty?'

'That'll be you next year,' Max says, getting all defensive.

'Cross that bridge then,' Trent says. 'Still in my twenties, as of tonight.'

Trent's apartment is as tiny as a council bylaw will allow. There's a shitter/shower combo tight off the kitchenette, and a bedroom with room for a bed and not much else. His living room, apart from a two-seater sofa and a television, is dominated by two large clothes horses stacked with wet laundry that fills the entire apartment with a mouldy stench. Trent picks up a sock from the horse and squeezes it in his hand.

'Been up a week. Still wet,' he sighs. 'I'd buy a dryer if I had space for it.'

He has a feel of some of the shirts, 'I'm gonna have to iron-dry one of these fuckers.'

'You should take it to a laundromat next time,' Max tells him.

'I'm not travelling on a fucken tram with a basket of wet clothes like some fucken pauper, Max,' Trent snaps.

He lifts a white shirt from the horse, lays it down on the grey carpet, and plugs in the iron. Max and I take both seats of his sofa.

'What do you think of my pad, Jackson?' Trent asks.

'It's central,' I say.

'Yep. Everything you could ever want, right on your doorstep. Rent's a fair bit, but if you think of it like a hotel room you clean yourself, it's not too bad.'

'Yeah, it's not too bad,' I say. 'If you think of it like that.'

'Anyway, drink up, boys. We're tearing up Chapel Street tonight,' Trent says, running his iron over his wet shirt.

'Ah, man,' Max goes, 'I'm not keen for clubs or anything like that. Just wanted a lowkey one. Don't need a song and dance for my birthday.'

Trent's shoulders twitch. He puts his iron down, stands up, and shoves an angry finger in Max's face.

'Listen here, you fuck. The day you have a chick on the go is the day you get to choose the fucken order of the night, alright?'

'Jesus Christ,' Max says. 'Calm down.'

'So, where's this one from?' I ask Trent as he recommences ironing duties.

'Girl from work. Said she was hitting up Chapel Street, and

I told her I was heading there myself.'

'Sounds like a solid plan,' I say.

'Yeah, well, hence we shouldn't fucken hang around here the whole fucken night discussing Max getting old. Let's fuck off after these beers and get on the ground in Chapel. Work it all out from there.'

****

We're six rounds in now. This Porcelain Peacock place is pretty desolate for a Saturday night, even though it's coming on ten. There are two girls sitting at a table in the corner, but their antipasto-platter and bread sticks scream at us to fuck off. The only other table that's occupied is filled with a pair of hustlers. Their words, not mine. Hustlers hustling. These blokes, all cut from the same fucken cloth. Pencil beards and puffy nipples poking through black V-neck fitted T's; spewing out words like tribe, and disruption, and passive income streams. Always drinking wine. If they dare engage me while I'm ordering my beer at the bar, I tell them that all wine tastes the same to me. Tastes like dead grapes. Always gets a rise out of them, that one does. Wine fucks. Though, no doubt later tonight, these same dare-to-dreamers will end up stumbling the corridors of Trent's apartment building trying to find the location of their early morning marketing meeting.

'She definitely said she was coming to this bar?' I ask Trent.

'She said this was one of her favourite bars,' he says. 'About a month back. As good a place to start as any.'

'Have you heard from her today, though?' I ask.

'You fucken amateur, Jackson,' Trent leans into me. 'You reckon I should give her even a hint I'm chasing? Fatal fucken error that. Best to play it cool in these situations. You've got some fucken catching up to do on these matters, mate. It's different times now.'

'I'm just a bit confused by this whole scenario,' I say. 'It's Max's birthday, and this place is more-or-less dead. It seems contrary to your usual style, that's all I'm saying.'

'What the fuck do you mean by my usual style?'

'All I'm asking for, is some clarification in regard to this seemingly loose rendezvous situation.'

'Fucken hell. Alright, then,' Trent says. 'So, I go to her, "Got any plans for the weekend?" She goes, "Maybe Chapel Street." I go, "Cool, where on Chapel Street?" She goes, "Don't know yet." And I remembered she told me she liked this place.'

One of Trent's legs starts shaking, and he starts picking hard at the label of his beer.

'As I said,' he continues, 'as good a place to start as any. And I doubt to fuck you'll be able to throw up a better plan.'

'Maybe send her a message to see where she's at,' I say. 'For pure logistical reasons.'

'Alright, calm down, you impatient fuck. I'll throw her one now.'

We're a few more rounds in, and the pair of hustlers a few tables over are really starting to get on my fucken nerves. Laughing and high fiving each other. Fucken cocky wine fucks. The two antipasto-platter chicks have parked up with them too, growing my utter disdain for the entire collective. My only comfort is my strong faith that their arrogance will be met with vengeance in some form or another. Life seldom lets these types of fucks go unpunished in my experience; the river always wants to return to level.

Trent's getting really agitated now, constantly checking his phone, so I throw some gasoline on the fire in order to chip away at his psych some more.

'Shouldn't she have messaged you back by now?' I ask.

Max's face rises from his handkerchief, 'Hard for her to write back when she's already got a dick in each hand.'

'Fucking relax, cunts!' Trent screams at us. 'I'll shoot her another one, then. Fucken impatient fucks.'

Max and I sit and drink our beers in silence while Trent types away on his phone longer than would seem normal. Max keeps yawning. Trent's muttering something under his breath about the poor cellular coverage of his provider.

And he's up out of his chair.

'Okay, okay. She's at Descent. Let's go, let's go!'

'Wait up,' I say. 'I'll take a quick piss before we go.'

'Fuck that, Jackson. Take it at the next bar. We need to go now. It's not far. I know a shortcut through a skatepark. Five-minute walk, tops.'

****

I'm finding it painful to walk. I'm bent over, hurting, my urethra in a constant state of contraction as my bladder tries its best not to piss my pants at twenty-fucken-nine-years-old. Every next club has a longer line, and there are no public toilets around this part of town since the council started to lock them all at night because of all the junkies with a penchant for shooting up in puddles of piss.

'Fucken hell. Is the club far from here?' I ask Trent through clenched teeth.

'It's further than I thought, to tell you the truth,' he says, looking down at his phone. 'It all looks the same to me, this fucken street.'

'I'm gonna fucken piss my pants, mate. I'm not even

kidding. Jesus Christ, Trent. How the fuck do you always get me into these fucken situations?'

Trent stops and points into the dark depths of a laneway.

'Piss on a wall, Jackson. Dogs do it all the fucken time and no one gives two fucks.'

'Fucken hell. Alright, you two wait here, then.'

I wander into the cobblestone laneway and find a shadow dark enough to grant me some semblance of privacy. I unzip against a wall, and heavenly streams fall from me. I close my eyes to savour the release.

A moment.

'Oi!'

A torch blinds me from further down the laneway. I hold one hand up to the light and chuck my dick back into my pants with the other. A wet patch grows on the inside of my undies due to my lack of shaking. Two cops emerge from behind the torch and walk towards me. Both blokes. One looks to be in his fifties. The other: barely out of his teens.

'Found ourselves a fucken pervert,' the younger one says.

'I'm sorry,' I say, holding both hands up. 'I tried to find a toilet, but I was—'

'Shut the fuck up, you filthy sack-of-shit,' the older one says. 'Name and address?'

'Jackson Young. 8 Windsor Close, Coburg.'

'You sure about that, cunt?' the younger one asks. 'It's a federal offence to provide false information to a Commonwealth official.'

'Yeah. I moved there recently, though. Yet to update my paperwork.'

'World's full of liars that look just like you, mate,' the older one says. 'Got a licence to back up your bullshit?'

I take out my wallet and hand him my driver licence. The older cop walks a few metres away, out of earshot, and I see him speak into the radio that's tethered to his stab proof vest. The younger one gets right up in my face, looking me up and down.

'You think the world wants to see your micro dick, Jackson?' he whispers in my ear.

'I was about to piss my pants, I swear to God.'

'God? You think old mate upstairs spent six days building this shit, just for you to go and spray your sick scent all over it?'

'It was the best I could do in the moment.'

'Best you could do in the moment,' he sighs, shaking his head. He takes out his gun from its holster. He squints one eye close and points the gun towards Chapel Street. I follow his line of sight across the road to a girl sitting at a tram stop with her head buried in her phone.

'See that one there?' he says. 'Exposed yourself to a young female, you did. You fucken sick fuck.'

'I'm up against the wall, angled away,' I say, my voice rising. 'She can't see my dick through my arse, can she?'

He turns back to me and runs the cold barrel of his gun up and down my cheek.

'Bout time you bite that fucken tongue of yours, Jacko,' he whispers. 'Indecent exposure. How you reckon that one will look when Trish from HR is thumbing through your résumé next time you find yourself between gigs. Skill set: fiddling with yourself in dark laneways. Mouth your way out of that one, ya fucken poet.'

The older cop walks over, and the younger one slides his gun back into its holster.

'Ran your name through our records,' the older one says. 'Your father was a Senior Sergeant?'

> You remember two days before the funeral
> Your mother showed you the newspaper
> Your daddy's famous now
> She said

'Yeah,' I say.

'You can't piss in public, Jackson. Not anymore,' he says in a voice now void of all aggression. He hands me back my licence. 'Don't do it again, mate.'

Chapter 19

The False Alibi

A penguin farts. On an ice shelf, in a snow storm, huddled on the edge of a colony trying to keep warm, a runt penguin farts. From an arsehole facing north, the stink wind hurtles through the frozen air, immediately losing all heat from its rectal origins. It gets colder and colder as it launches over the white caps of the Southern Ocean, gathers speed over Bass Strait, bounces off the chilly waters of Port Phillip Bay, and is only stopped by my face.

We're standing in line for Descent. We've been waiting, not moving, for nearly twenty minutes now. Idiots in front, creeps behind, with a nasty southerly battering us from the side. Finally, there's a slight shuffle up the line, and we inch slowly closer towards the fat fuck checking IDs at the door.

'You and your fucken bladder, Jackson,' Trent says. 'You know how girls like to bounce around bars. We'll end up playing cat and mouse all fucken night now.'

'I told you I wanted to take a piss back at the bar, didn't I. Nearly pissed my pants. Fucken nearly got arrested too, thanks to you.'

'Well, if those pig cunts minded their own fucken business once-in-a-while, we'd already be inside by now,' Trent says.

'Maybe we should just call it a night,' Max says. 'Go get a bite to eat. I feel like I might be coming down with something. Anyone else feeling hot?'

'It's your fucken birthday,' Trent says. 'We're staying out and getting wasted. Not having you bail on us now, you flaky cunt.'

'It'll be alright once we're in, mate,' I say to Max, then turn to Trent. 'Who's this girl from work, anyway? She got a name yet?'

'You're not having a crack, Jackson!'

'Calm down, mate. I'm just asking what her deal is. Curious of the social dynamic, that's all.'

'Her name is Phoebe. She's extremely attractive, but she's also the smartest one at work. By a long fucken way too. I figure her advanced level of intellect will help her see through all the fake superficial shit in this world.'

'And fall for a genuine down-to-earth guy like you?' I ask.

'Yes, Jackson,' Trent hisses. 'Like me.' His shoulders twitch, and he shoves a finger in my face. 'Don't you even think about fucking this one up for me.'

****

We're in. Jagged a booth in the corner above the sunken dancefloor. We're sitting drinking our beers with little to offer the passing other than civil smiles and the fading scent of our cologne that is most likely drowned out by smoke machine residual anyway.

We've gone another two rounds each, and Trent still hasn't sighted Phoebe. He chucked her another message, but he reckons this nightclub has thick concrete walls and claims the message mightn't've got through to her. He tells us he's going to fuck off his current cellular provider come Monday morning. His eyes keep dancing around all corners of the nightclub. Every now-and-then, he gets up and stands on his seat, a meercat atop of his mound.

And he does.

He spots her

'Fucken got her! At the bar,' he says. 'Come on, boys.'

'You go, Trent,' Max says. 'Bring her and her lot back here. We'll hold the fort for ya.'

'Fuck, Max. You really can be a cunt when you want to be, can't you,' Trent says. 'I'm not going to fucken rock up to her one-up like some fucken loser. You two fucken cunts are coming with me. But stand behind me. And don't even fucken think about saying anything.'

With no alternative to offer, Max and I surrender our booth as per Trent's wishes. We weave between the crowd, working our way towards the bar. Trent approaches Phoebe, stealth like, and taps her on the shoulder. She jumps a little bit out of her skin and turns around. She's about five foot nothing in heels, a redhead turned blonde I believe, and looks to have only recently escaped her teens.

'Oh hey, Trent,' and she gives him a restrained side-on hug with a light pat on the back.

'Chartreuse?' he asks.

'Ah, yeah, sure?'

'Cool, cool. These are my two mates from school. Awful humans,' he says, thumbing at us over his shoulder. 'Don't reach into that cage.'

'Hi,' she says.

'Hi,' we say back to her.

Trent gives us a dirty look as if to say, 'that's enough chat from you two.' He turns around and starts straddling the bar to get served, leaning right across it, waving his finger furiously at the bartenders. And a six-foot-two, flat cap with a tattooed sleeve walks right up next to Phoebe.

'Jason,' she says, 'this is Trent from work.'

Flat Cap reaches across her and crushes Trent's hand with a violent handshake.

'How do you two know each other?' Trent asks, all accusatory.

'Actually,' she says, smiling up at Flat Cap. 'We just met tonight, waiting in the line to get in.'

Trent's head turns to me with reptilian ill, and his eyes sharpen at mine. Some bartender bloke leans his ear across the bar, 'Yeah, what ya having, mate?'

'Two Chartreuse! Green!'

The music is so fucken loud in this joint that Trent has to hold up two fingers to clarify the quantity, and the bartender reaches up to the top shelf for the alchemy of two French monks. From where Max and I stand, we can see Flat Cap gently rub the small of Phoebe's back while the bartender pours Trent's two Chartreuse shots.

'Cheers,' Trent says.

'Cheers,' Phoebe says.

Both shot glasses are slammed down empty on the bar. Flat Cap catches Phoebe's eye and nods to the exit. She turns to Trent.

'Looks like we're gonna bounce, but I'll see you at work on Monday. Cool?'

'Yep,' Trent says.

Flat Cap gives us all a little nod, and she leads him by his hand towards the front door.

****

Our booth has been snaked by three pastel-shirted dickheads while we were at the bar, so we're forced to stand awkwardly on the rise above the sunken dancefloor. The three of us, leering over the swarm of sweaty filth moving to music who are all desperately trading in a currency that's bleeding out on them by the day. Trent looks devastated, staring down at the dancefloor with his mouth open, as if Flat Cap has walked out with his wife, his kids, family holidays, his first home, and a backyard barbeque on a scorcher of a Christmas day.

Trent's first to break the silence.

'You and your fucken bladder, Jackson,' he says, shaking his head.

'Sometimes my mind can get a bit ahead of itself too, mate,' I reply.

And Trent grabs my throat.

'Don't you ever fucken think you're better than me,' he screams in my face. 'Fucken ever, you fucken faggot. Got it?'

> The toilet seat was up
> Don't fool yourself, you fucken idiot
> You know what this means

And only when Trent's mad eyes see that I've heard him loud and clear, does he release his grip. I rub my throat and look at Max. He looks horrified at the whole thing but says fuck all. It hurts to swallow. The pain makes me aware of how much spit I must swallow all the time because now it's hurting like hell each time I do.

'Fuck this,' I say. 'I'm done with all this fucken carry on. What are you keen for, Max? Still up for a feed?'

'We waited so long in the line,' he says. 'Paid the door

charge too. Skin in the game now.'

'Fuck it, fine,' I say.

Trent just keeps leering at the dancefloor, taking long sips of his beer. Pitch black must be the darkness of that cat's thoughts.

****

Rather than throw good money after bad and fork out for a ride all the way back to fucken Coburg, I've decided I'll catch a late-night train. I'm taking the shortcut through Lovers Walk, a poorly lit thoroughfare full of rubbish and excrement that traces the train tracks behind the arse ends of bars and clubs towards South Yarra Station. The whole walk is covered head to toe in street art; or what it *should* be called: vandalism. I'm feeling a bit crook now from all the drink. Septic spew stews deep. I put one hand on the spray-paint splattered wall to steady myself, my head heavy, saliva pooling in the front of my mouth. I dry wretch. An unemotional tear escapes my eye, and I end its run quickly with the back of my hand.

Where do you think she is right now?

Chelsea

There's someone walking towards me, a girl, so I stand up straight and try to swallow all thought of throwing up.

'Jackson?'

She stops.

It's Georgia, one of Chelsea's friends. They look alike, the two of them. It's the blond hair. Means they always get mistaken for sisters. In a weird way, it's comforting to see her, a physical presence from a life that is starting to seem nothing more than a trick of the mind; like some dream you remember when you first get out of bed but has escaped recall by the time you step out of the shower; and yet, at the same time, it inflames the growing sickness in my gut.

'How's things?' Georgia asks.

'Yeah, good.'

'And Chelsea?'

'Chelsea?' I ask.

'How's Chelsea? I haven't seen her in a while.'

'We ended things a couple of weeks back.'

'I'm sorry, Jackson. I had no idea. I haven't spoken to her in a few months.'

'You haven't?'

'We had a bit of a falling out a while back.'

'She never mentioned that.'

'Are you okay, though? I thought you two were so good together.'

'Yeah, I'm fine. These things happen, don't they. It's hard these days, for two people to stay on the same path. It's different times now.'

'Yeah, I know. But I thought you two would be the ones who would. Anyway, I better get going. I'm running late to meet a friend.'

'Yeah, I've got a train to catch too.'

'But it's good to see you, Jackson. I hope I'll still get to see you around. Melbourne's a small town in a weird way.'

'Yeah, for sure.'

Go on

Ask it

Georgia wanders off down the dark path.

I call out after her.

'Georgia!'

She stops.

'Yeah?'

'You and Chelsea. What did you have your falling out over?'

'It'll sound stupid.'

'No, it won't.'

She looks at the ground, 'I shouldn't say.'

'I'm just trying to make sense of a few things, that's all.'

'She's still my friend, though. I feel bad talking about her behind her back.'

'Yeah, it's okay. I understand.'

Georgia turns and walks away, but she stops after a few paces and turns back.

'She skipped my birthday dinner because she said she was too tired from work. Maybe I made a bigger deal of it than what it was. I knew she was being hit with some long hours at work at the time. But still, it was my birthday, you know? One night a year.'

'Yeah, I remember that night,' I say. 'Okay, thanks.'

'I probably sound like a lunatic to you.'

'Nah, it's all good.'

'The thing is, Chelsea does what Chelsea wants. She's always been like that. Anyway, I'm sure you figured that one out early.'

And we both go our separate ways. I do remember that night. Clearly, in fact. Chelsea told me it was a 'girls only' thing. I remember she was all excited to go out, done up all beautiful.

You will know

His name

And what I do fucken know is this: Chelsea left out the door that night for Georgia's birthday party.

Chapter 20

Vulgar Sore

'I am sick **of** the showy seeming
Of a life that is half a lie;
Of the faces lined with scheming
In the throng that hurries by.'
John Boyle O'Reilly, d. 1890.

Monday morning, closing in on eight. Back to reality, early to work. Deep in clauses and subclauses and case studies. After my relatively early retirement Saturday night, I've spent way too much time with my own thoughts, so I'm thankful for the distraction the workday presents.

Yesterday, Max spent his whole day in bed apart from getting up around two-in-the-afternoon to destroy the bathroom with a paint-stripping shit that kindly crawled itself down the hallway and into my room. Trent's throat tickle left a large bruise too. When I sat down at my desk before, Will asked if it was a hickey. I had to tell him it was chaffing from the collar of my wetsuit after a Sunday surf at Philip Island. That shut him up, thank fuck.

My boss is pacing nervously. He made me move desks this morning. Kicked me into the spare desk next to the frosted doors and made everyone shuffle one desk over. Said it was so the new start could be seated closest to his office so that he could answer any questions she might have. Dita is her name. 'Greek,' my boss said. 'Shorthand for something longer.'

****

She turns up just before nine. Of course, she's the girl with the black hair and the big blue eyes that smile all the time. Nothing pisses me off more in this world than the sheer predictability of shit people, though, in this rare exception, I'm glad my boss gave her the job. He begins with the initial introductions.

'Okay, Dita,' my boss says. 'So, we have one account manager away on holiday. Rick. He's in Bali. Lucky him. He's the one old enough to be your grandfather. Which leaves these two jokers here. This is Will. We like to think of him as the office pet,' and he laughs at his own stand-up. 'And Jackson here, he's our resident under-the-thumber. Good luck getting him out of the house.'

Watch this, cunt.

'Actually, Carl, I should correct you there,' I say. 'My relationship, much like your very own, has come to a sudden and abrupt end in recent weeks.'

'I'm—I'm sorry to hear that, Jackson,' he says.

I can tell I've thrown him completely off his game. His eyes dart towards Dita to read her reaction which is nothing more than warm confusion. I show my palms to my boss.

'Thanks, Carl. I appreciate your concern, but it's all for the best.' And I turn to Dita, 'We were together six years. Utmost respect for her, but sometimes you just need to do your own thing. It's something you feel, you know, deep down in your guts.' And she smiles. 'Plus, I'm still in my twenties,' and I turn to look Carl in the eye. 'No kids, either. So, no harm, no foul.'

And I can tell the fat old fuck wants to belt me right now, but, as he so clearly stated in our one-on-one meeting just over a week ago, Violence will not be tolerated in the workplace, Jackson.

****

He's spent most of the morning hovering around Dita's desk. Leaning all over her, his bloated sausage fingers resting on the top of her chair as he explains the intricacies of our account management program, Destiny—of which I know a fuck load more about than him. I saw her, more than once, turn her head away from his gingivitis coffee breath in barely disguised disgust. If this creepy manipulative fuck considers himself an alpha in the artificial corporate structure of this sadistic fucken company, I'm going to do my best to assure him that no, this is very much not the case. Not in the tangible world beyond the logo on the frosted doors.

Your walls aren't real, Carl.

You fucken cunt.

He riled me up a bit at our team meeting earlier this morning, my boss did. He stood at the head of the boardroom table, looked each one of us in the eye, and asked us to bring our full self to work. Clearly, he has no understanding of the words he uttered because if we were to do what he asked, the building would be ablaze within an hour.

****

He's back again. Now he's sat his fat arse down on the corner of Dita's desk, and he's telling her about all the lunch spots close to our office.

'You look like you take care of yourself, Dita. There's a salad bar called Salivating Salads a block over. And a smoothie joint not far from here too. Sometimes I just have a smoothie for lunch, when I'm having a cleansing week. And there's an organic vegan café that does a great quinoa, tofu, and cabbage salad. It sounds horrible, but trust me, it's not. I like to have the odd vegan day from time to time, to let my digestive system rest.'

Half a belt notch down and the cunt's granting himself health guru status. It's a setup, this conversation is. Without a shred of doubt, this small talk is groundwork so his imminent invitation to lunch doesn't come across as too forward. Something like, 'Oh, Dita, that spot I was telling you about earlier, heading there now. You've gotta try their Caesar salad. It's fucken amazing. Grab your coat, we'll beat the lunch rush.'

Scheming old fat fuck.

Fuck him.

I walk over to break up their conversation.

'How ya finding things, Dita?' I ask, barely acknowledging my boss.

'Yeah, good. Still getting my head around it all,' she says, smiling.

'Yep, there's a lot to take in here, that's for sure.'

'Everyone seems really nice, though.'

'Yeah, well, yell out if you have any questions,' I say. 'Or if you wanna grab lunch.'

'Hope you like burgers,' my boss scoffs.

'It's a mince sandwich,' I reply. 'That's all it fucken is.'

97

'I brought my own in today,' Dita says. 'Sunday leftovers.'

'Oh yep,' I say. 'No dramas.'

'But later in the week, let's do it,' she says.

I sit down at my desk knowing I've done enough to at least upset my boss's rhythm for the time being. I'm feeling quite satisfied with what I've accomplished today.

'And remember, Dita,' my boss says. 'My door is always open.'

'Finally install some fucken hinges, Carl?' I yell out from my desk.

Honestly, I don't know what the fuck my boss does in his office all day. Ex-wife stalking no doubt. About once a month, he sends us some by-the-numbers, motivational essay that he's stumbled upon. Usually a basterdised, dumb downed rip-off of some Greek cunt I learnt about when I was eight. And for this shit service that I'm unable to unsubscribe from, the arsehole probably takes home triple my wage. Most will be syphoned away on child support now, at least there's some fucken karma left in this world, yet even when that is factored in, he will still make bigger bank than me by weeks end. Fuck him. I take extra comfort knowing he can do nothing about how I acted before. That this corporate environment he exploits also inhibits him, as all I did per se was act cordial to a new workmate. I mean, I do wish the bloke all the best. I'm honest when I say that. He can go speed dating or online dating or maybe meet a new partner through some state-sponsored community outreach programme for fucked up over-forty divorcees. But if for a second, he thinks he's going to get one-up on his ex-wife by hooking up with a girl like Dita, then he truly fails to understand the order of things. And really, I didn't need to do anything anyway because there was no chance he was going to get anywhere anyway. Not in any place outside his fucken mind that is. But I felt obliged to clarify the matter. To give him a message, loud and clear: No, you fuck, you don't. And maybe it wasn't the best career move ever, but if that promotion gets me even one step closer to turning into what he is, then I couldn't give a fuck about anything anymore. The first time I get Dita alone, I'm going to tell her what happened the night of my boss's birthday drinks and describe—in graphic detail—exactly how wrinkled and withered his dick and sack is.

Chapter 21
Blind Carbon Copy

Wednesday. We're sitting in a café down a laneway off Little Collins. Dita and me. We have a small table for two, inside the front window that looks out at the heavy lunchtime foot traffic. The room is filled with the rich aroma of coffee that I'm told, by scrawled chalk, is sustainably sourced from plantations in Haiti. There's a wall of all brick down one side, and a large communal table at the back packed with ravenous entrepreneurs. Their heads between headphones, buried heavy in their keyboards as they work away in solitude building their global empires.

'I like your eyes, Jackson.'

'Thanks.'

'Green's my favourite colour, you know?'

Some poet mate with ratty hair and a wrist tatt returns with our two dishes. Dita's ordered a smoked salmon salad. I've chosen this platter thing from the specials board that has a bit of this and that on it, though, I feel I've paid overs when Poet Mate slams it down in front of me and I see how little is presented on my plate. Everything's on special in this town and everything's still so fucken expensive.

'I think we're similar, you and me,' Dita says.

'What makes you think that?'

'I have a sense for these things.'

'Okay.'

'Do you like music, Jackson?'

'The odd time it's done right.'

'I like music. And sounds, speeches, spoken word. My ear likes all that stuff. I make these montages at home. I record beats, muck around with loops. Sometimes I record myself speaking. I take the words, and sounds, and beats, and play with it all. Try out different effects. Try to place it all in some sort of order. Make sense of all the noise, you know.'

'Sounds cool,' I say, impaling a slice of radish with my fork. 'So, where did you work before you came to us?'

'This finance group, down in Docklands,' she says.

'Why'd you leave there?'

'Why does anyone leave?'

'For something better?'

'Yes,' she sighs. 'For something better.'

'So, what do you think of it so far?'

'It seems like an alright place to work. So far.'

'You're half there. It's a place to work.'

'How long have you been with them for?'

'Seven years,' I say. 'It'll be seven in November. Does the job, pays the bills. But nearly seven years and not one pay rise once. So, don't hold your breath. There's this team leader role that should rightfully be mine already, but Carl's been dragging his feet announcing it. Keeps sliding down his priority list. He's got a few personal problems burning in the background, though. Wife binned him a couple of months back. Ran off with her personal trainer. He didn't take it too well if you want to know the whole story.'

'You know it's a form of control?'

'What is?'

'These people, companies. They keep you in a state of static. Look how they set salaries for our generation. Just enough to live, right? To live some level of comfort. Enough for all your problems to seem first world at least. Enough for you to feel some sense of guilt whenever you complain. But never enough to get ahead. Never enough that you can well and truly tell your boss to go fuck himself if need be. So, you can't leave until you find something better. We all still need food and shelter. It's a very primal form of control when you think about it.'

'Orangutan theory,' I say.

'What's that?'

'When you watch orangutans swing in the trees, they don't let go of one branch until they have a firm grip on another.'

'Because they're scared of the fall?'

'Or what's waiting for them on the forest floor.'

'Anyway,' she goes. 'It pays to at least be aware of how strongly we're tethered to the system. That team leader role? Carl told me in my interview that if I play my cards right, and get through my probation period, then it could be mine in six-months' time.'

'He did, did he?'

'Now look at his smart little setup. He's got the two of us working hard, not questioning back. Biting tongues. That promotion is just around the corner, right? We'll work every day to within an inch of our sanity. Too exhausted in the evening to consider much more than dinner and bed. Hardly worth the bother, really.'

Fucken sack-of-shit fat fuck creep cunt.

'Well, Carl's lost his fucken mind if he thinks he can play me like that,' I say, dropping my fork loudly on my plate.

'For God's sake, don't tell him I told you. I'm on probation, remember.'

'Yeah, okay, fine.'

'Promise?'

'Promise.'

'I think about this stuff a lot,' she continues. 'How it's hard to give thought to a melting iceshelf when you're going home with a migraine every day. And I feel bad about that, you know? Wakes me up early sometimes.'

'How's your lunch?' I ask.

'Good. Yours?'

'Average,' I say, glaring at Poet Mate.

'So, I'm gonna let you in on a little secret—Sorry, I hope my chat isn't weirding you out, I've been accused before of being an over-sharer.'

'Nah, it's all good. Fire away.'

'So, I have a boyfriend.'

Of course.

'We've been together since our first year of Uni. Five years, first love and all that. But I'm not going to reveal this to Carl.'

'Why?'

'Because it's none of his business, first and foremost. And why take away his rope. You don't think I saw right through his little lunch spot spew. You reckon he'd plant his arse on the corner of your desk, Jackson? I see everything with so much clarity that if he even had half a clue to the depth of my vision, he would have been way too terrified to hire me.'

'Jesus.'

'So, Jackson. Any dark stories from your past?'

'Not really.'

'You can tell me another time, then. You wanna know why I left my last job?'

'Yeah, go on.'

'My previous boss, he was this old guy. Should have been retired a decade ago, but he liked the taste of his pay check. I had him as gay the first couple of weeks on the job. Very flamboyant, wrists flying in all directions. Then I found out he had a wife, kids, even a grandchild. He was very tactile too, so I considered for a moment he was just a classic closet case. A tragic by-product of being born in some dustbowl up north. But then came the suggestive innuendo, and I could see straight through the sick fuck in an instant. Flamboyance was his mask. So, I started recording him. Every day when he approached my desk, I pressed record on my phone as soon as I saw him approach. Then I took everything that fell from his mouth, I took it home and added music, and loops, and beats, and started building this montage. And so forth and so on. You know, I started looking for another job as soon as I was on to his play. But it's hard out there, in these times, to find something straight away. Sometimes there's no other branch. So, on and on it continued, and every day my montage grew longer and longer.'

She looks out the window, packed with suits and heels pounding the footpath.

'Is that the story?' I ask.

'Then, Carl offered me this job. And now, I've got a choice: I have this montage of my old boss, closing in on two hours. I can either go quietly or—in my grand finale—I could send the audio montage out companywide and Bcc the fucker's wife.'

And I'm in love.

She stares down at the wad of smoked salmon on her fork, dripping with pesto.

'So, what did you do?' I ask.

'In the end, nothing.'

'Why?'

'I wasn't sure if I wanted the consequences on my conscience, you know. I couldn't unsend it once it was sent. He has a wife and kids. And a grandchild. So, I did nothing. But knowing I can still ruin his life at any moment I choose, that's enough for me. For now. Why? If you were me, what would you do?'

'It would have already been sent.'

'So, that's where we're different,' she says with those smiling blue eyes.

Chapter 22

Session Three

Jesus Christ. She's had some running repairs done to her hair. Probably stormed back into the suburban stylist spewing about last week's hack job and demanded for it to be fixed for free. Poor cunt with the scissors just forced to cut away at it some more, a patch job over small talk. A couple of auburn highlights have been added in what's left of the fringe. Complete, utter, mess, all of it. She's better off shaving her whole head and starting again, as far as I'm concerned.

'Tell me a little bit more about yourself, Jackson.'

'What would you like to know?'

'What makes you angry?'

'People.'

'Why do they make you angry?'

'You can't trust them.'

'All of them?'

'A fair number of them.'

'Why does this make you angry, Jackson?'

'Because they make you doubt the ones you should.'

'Should people trust you, Jackson?'

'Yes.'

'Why? Are you so pure? Do you never lie?'

'Not about the important stuff.'

'Do you think you would want to know every truth, though? If you were all seeing and all knowing, do you think you would want it? Maybe some lies make the world more palatable?'

'How can you make the right decisions without knowing the truth, though?'

'Do you believe it's your right to know all?'

'I believe it's my right to know it if I need it.'

'Tell me more.'

'Some people, they come at you. And I'm a firm believer in revenge. There's a time and place for vengeance in every situation, as far as I'm concerned.'

'By vengeance, do you mean violence?'

'No.'

'Are you ready to talk about the incident?'

'Not really, to be honest.'

'Why?'

'Because, then—I'd rather move on with things.'

'You want to forget what happened?'

'Yes. That is what I want.'

'Why?'

'Because I don't want to think about it.'

'But you do remember what I told you about pain in our last session, don't you?'

'Yes.'

'And still, you don't want to talk about it?'

'No, it's not what I want. If I talk about it, I'll think about it. That's not what I want, no.'

'Talking takes away its power, Jackson.'

'But it doesn't change anything.'

'It can change your perception of it.'

'But it's not all in my fucken head!' I yell at her.

For once, her pen stops scribbling in her little notepad.

I bring my volume back down to civil.

'It's not all in my head,' I say. 'Things do exist outside it. You do know that, don't you? Or did you wag that lecture at psych school?'

'Do you have dark thoughts, Jackson?'

'No.'

'Never?'

'Most of the time, no, I don't.'

'But sometimes?'

'So, what? So too does everyone.'

'They don't go away on their own, Jackson. You need to find a way to cleanse them from your being, before they become part of you.'

'This is fucken garbage, this is.'

'You're getting angry now.'

'Yes, you're correct. Top marks to you. I'm getting angry. It's my fucken right to get angry at things I don't like. This fucken world sometimes.'

'But now your anger is controlling you.'

'Fuck you. What would you know?'

'See…'

'Fucken garbage, the shit that comes out of your mouth. Bet you go home to some fucken lanky arsehole, iron him some shapeless checked shirt and a pair of camel chinos, throw some tongs and an apron at him and tell him to go tend the barbie while you entertain your other fucken sad friends with shit wine you bought in bulk online. Hourlong conversations about convection ovens. Year after year, until all your friends fuck off their marriages one by one, until it's just you and him, and then you yourself start to doubt that shiny piece of dirt shit on your finger cos your fucken sleazebag ballroom dancing instructor gave you a wink while your husband's back was turned when he spun you the wrong way and fucked up your foxtrot.'

'Jackson, can you tell me how the events of that Friday night three weeks ago affected you emotionally?'

'As a matter of fact, it made me a little upset. If some fucken honesty is what you're after.'

'That's your time up, Jackson.'

'Good.'

'This was also your final session covered by your corporate health plan. If you wish to continue, please talk to my receptionist on your way out, and she'll run you through your payment options moving forward.'

I tell the receptionist to go fuck herself on my way out, and I walk out into the dark laneway. It's pissing down from above. Heavy droplets from high clouds that hide the tops of skyscrapers thunder down with full force, forming river rapid drains. I cop a soaking as I make my way down Elizabeth Street, weaving between the swarming sea of umbrellas whose sharp corners hunt for my eyes. My winter coat is fast becoming waterlogged, so I walk into some dollar junk shop and purchase a black umbrella. I open it outside, and the strong southerly catches it immediately, snapping the metal ribs, so I walk all the way down to Flinders St Station with my deformed umbrella acting as my sole shelter from the open heavens.

Chapter 23

Home

More train delays. Crowds stand a dozen deep on the platform. I've stopped seeing faces. Stopped seeing them the way I used to. Everyone around me, their faces, they're not made of skin anymore. In front of who they are, blocking the world's sight, is a wire mesh smeared in crude plaster to the shape of a face. Creatures with features painted on. Plastic eyes. Masks that hide their hate that lies beneath. And all their words, a cacophony, so distant from their true thoughts, rise and rise and steam as white noise in the cold winter air.

My train to Coburg finally pulls into the platform at Flinders, and at least three trains' worth of waiting commuters surge into the one, each person scrambling in front of the other, jostling to claim their precious seat for their long ride home to sit on their sofas. I walk at a brisk yet civil pace towards the carriage doors, but every arsehole sees the half opening I give them and takes it. And now I'm the one who's being crunched against the doors as they close in on me. The train shakes on the tracks and grows towards full speed. The air is dense, filled with condensation rising from waterlogged clothes. My feet slip about in the puddles fast forming from all the dripping umbrellas as I try to find a handhold between the hives of fingers wrapped around every pole and grip within arm's reach. At this time of day, in these less than ideal circumstances, fake faces begin to fall, and they all, one by one, fail to disguise their utmost disgust at each other's existence. Stuck in this tomb of torture, with all personal space encroached, time slows until there is too much of it. This endless time, tense and torn, leads to too much thinking.

I would have been home hours ago.

By now, back then.

Stop.

The train empties at every station but never enough to be free of a stranger's breath in my face. Every vacated seat is swarmed on in an instant by young and old. Ravenous seagulls fighting over the last rotting penguin carcass. The train driver comes across the beat-up speaker system, its distortion attacking my ears.

'Apologies for the delay, passengers. There's been another obstruction on the tracks. We hope to get moving as soon as possible. We sincerely apologise for any inconvenience this may cause you tonight.'

An old lady with bright beads hanging off a face of melted wax, rolls her plastic eyes and leans in towards me.

'They really need to do something about this appalling public transport network,' she says.

There's no ring on her wedding finger.

I get closer to her still.

In a slow and articulate voice, I say to her, 'Let us not pretend, for one moment, that either of us, truly, has anywhere better to be than here.'

Her fake face molds itself into fear, and she scampers off towards the door to the next carriage, looking back over her shoulder twice to ensure that I'm not following behind. I hold a big grin back at her until she's gone. At least I'm honest. Some people just don't want to hear the truth. They're terrified of it, clearly. I feel the train engage the tracks, and once again we're moving.

****

I open Max's front door, and I'm hit by a stench of rotting flesh. My jaw spasms at the putrid smell that assaults me: expired chicken floating in a bowl of curdled milk. I walk into the living room and see a muscular body, with a shaved head and a bushman's beard, lying prone on the sofa, using the three tattered cushions as both a pillow and a blanket. Legs so long they hang over the arm rest by at least a foot. Only a slight snore signifies life. There's a khaki duffel bag on the floor beside the glass coffee table. It doesn't look much like him, but I know it is. Fucken Lazarus.

Chapter 24
The Ballad of Belarus

It all started going downhill for Bones about six months ago, around the start of the Northern Hemisphere winter. He's over in Belarus, two hours north of Minsk, living in this tiny little apartment with his wife, their son, and her parents. It was a one bedder, but her folks had the one bedroom, so Bones and his two mouths had to make do with a mattress on the cold tiled floor beside the kitchen, an area originally intended for dining. Neither of her parents spoke a word of English, and even his wife spoke broken at best, so the whole spousal sponsoring setback with Australian immigration failed to translate with much clarity to his new in-laws.

Money was tight all round.

His father-in-law was a frail, grizzled alcoholic who ran a start-up in backyard dentistry. Bones came home one morning to find a blue tarp on the sofa and his father-in-law's knee on some transient dude's forehead. One hand was ripping out a rotten tooth with a pair of pliers while the other was splashing his patient's face with a bottle of vodka.

His mother-in-law was a tea reading, reiki practising, sack-of-shit spiritualist whose main hustle was foretelling the futures of some of the ten thousand living in the surrounding six estates. This service was charged by the hour, of course, though it did include a complimentary onceover with her magic hands.

Bones's new wife, despite having a Master of Laws from Melbourne University, found it impossible to get anything other than temp work in the current climate. This lack of regular income curbed all thought of Bones and her getting a place of their own.

Bones himself, after his failed flirtation with Belarussian Real Estate Ltd, was stuck in perpetual unemployment with his limited language skills. Until some ticket guy at the local train station, who was a massive fan of the film Crocodile Dundee, sorted him out with that train cleaning gig. His shift started ten-at-night, and he had to work through until five-in-the-morning, cleaning vomit and piss off late night train carriages, getting them all ready for the morning commute to Minsk. When he wasn't working or sleeping, Bones would spend time playing soccer with his young son, who liked nothing more than kicking a ball around with his dad in the small park in the middle of the six estates.

Anyway, everyone tolerated each other in the confined space for the first couple of years, but Bones sensed the contempt of his mother-in-law growing. So, it's last December, on the approach to Christmas, and his mother-in-law's brother shot a bear in the woods up in Siberia or wherever. Bones comes home one morning to find its leg and arse stuffed in the freezer.

'Get us through winter,' his mother-in-law told him.

On Christmas Day, she served up some bear broth made from the foot. Bones merely intimated that his appetite wasn't the strongest that evening, and his mother-in-law lost her fucken mind at that. Threw a full bowl of the broth straight at his head. Bones ducked, and it bounced off the wall, splattering liquified dead bear across the mattress that he slept on with his wife and son.

'You fucken scrape shit off trains, but you're too good to eat my food, you ungrateful fat cunt,' his mother-in-law screamed at him in Belarussian. His poor little son started crying at all the shouting, so Bones was like, 'Fuck this shit,' and he grabbed his long coat and his ushanka hat and stormed out into the snowy night. His thinking was to take a quick stroll around the block to clear his head, to give his mother-in-law some space to calm down and all that. But he was enjoying his own company so much he kept on going, beyond the six estates, to see where the streets would lead him. After a few hours, he found himself caught up in a maze of cold concrete in a nearby town, and with the temperature plummeting into the healthy negatives, Bones thought it was probably time to circle back to the apartment. As he did, he passed an alleyway and heard a noise. Intriguing enough for him to stop and stare down into its dark depths. He walked towards it: the light and the noise. Shoes scraping on a wooden floor. Closer still. The battering of pads. Through the bars on the window he saw little extravagance. A basic boxing ring, a bench press, a few dumbbells, a couple of skipping ropes. Probably some community project Gorbachev signed off on, back in the day. Still, on that cold Christmas night, all alone in Belarus, that gym shone out to Bones like a beacon of heaven and hope. And from that day forth, every hour he wasn't picking up used frangers from between train seats, he'd be at the gym; getting in shape, getting bigger, working on his jabs, crosses, hooks, and uppercuts.

Not that his home life improved in any way whatsoever. Apparently, his mother-in-law sat down with her cup of Twinings one morning and read in the leaves that Bones would betray her daughter, which came pretty fucken conveniently close on the back of his Christmas Day culinary critique. And day by day, the stale air of the apartment grew more and more tense. His wife too, started to throw him more and more shade after her mother's mystic revelation, so the whole ill atmosphere only drove Bones's dedication to the gym harder. It was there, after work one morning, he met some massive fucken monster who told him about this new form of synthetic steroid that triples your gains overnight. Bones is like, 'I'm twenty-nine, my life is fucked. Rack it up, Viktor!' So, every day for the next couple of months, Viktor would load up a syringe and ram it into one of Bones's arse cheeks. And Bones exploded in size. Then he downed some fat stripping drugs that his new mate stole from some horse stables, and his transformation was complete.

It's the start of the European summer now. Bones and Viktor had become the best of mates, and when they weren't shattering personal bests on the bench, or breaking each other's nose in the ring, they were rooting strippers at a bar across the road from their gym. Bones's allegiance to monogamy had been all but destroyed by a quarterback in a cornfield a few years back. His chat-up line to the strippers was to tell them he owns a flash apartment on Bondi Beach and that he's tight mates with Russell Crowe. Did the trick most of the time.

'G'day, dah'lin. Ever seen the movie *Gladiator*?'

Anyway, believe it or not, Bones was actually enjoying life for a little while. Then, one morning, he woke up with an extremely swollen arse cheek. And over the next few days it grew some more, and it started smelling, and then it started leaking. A boil full of ooze that he would try to milk awkwardly in the mirror, looking back over his shoulder at his septic arse in the tiny sole bathroom of the apartment while his mother-in-law hammered on the door, yelling at him to hurry the fuck up. But every day it just kept haemorrhaging more and more gunk. Bit of red at first, but then it thickened and turned a vibrant yellow. Turns out Australia and Belarus don't have a reciprocal health care policy, so Bones had to take the project upon himself to fix. Methylated spirits to kill the infection, a dousing of Brut for Men to mask the smell. It did little to help. Compounding the matter, he was also copping continued resentment from his wife, his mother-in-law, and even his father-in-law the odd time the old cunt was conscious. Therefore, Bones decided he had no other option but to employ his evacuation plan. Problem was, his passport was locked away in a safe, deep in the closet of his in-law's bedroom, and his line of credit had been decimated to only a couple of hundred dollars. So first, he contacted the Australian embassy in Poland and declared his passport stolen and listed the boxing gym as his residential address. But now, that was his credit card maxed out. So, he started dating a stripper behind his wife's back, on pretence that he'd take her back to Australia and get her a role in *Gladiator 2*. Bones knew full well that strippers are paid in cash, and seldom—in any city or any country—does this cash ever find its way into banks, for fear of it then finding its way into the hands of the taxman, who will blow it all on baby incubators and walking frames for the elderly. Bones got lucky with Svetlana the Stripper. She didn't even worry about a safe. Kept all her lappy cash right under her mattress.

When his new passport finally arrived, Bones threw it straight in his locker at the gym, where it would stay safe and secure until the time was right.

So, that takes us all the way up to Wednesday evening, the one just gone. Bones took his little son for one last kick around the park in the middle of the six estates, and when it came time for the two of them to go upstairs for dinner, Bones dropped down on his knee, gave his son a big long hug, then cupped his little face.

'Sorry to do this to ya, mate,' he said. 'I'll come back for you one day, I promise.'

Bones left for his graveyard shift that night. On his way out, he slid a note under the door that went someway to explaining his actions. First, he stopped by the gym to pick up his passport, then he went over to Svetlana's house. He quickly threw one up her, and while she was showering he cleared out all the cash from under her mattress and left out the front door, hailing the first ride he could find to Minsk International, where he chucked a large wad of Belarusian rouble on the counter in exchange for a one-way ticket back to Melbourne. And when he took his middle seat on the thirty-eight hour, four-stop long haul—the stench of his bleeding, pus-filled arse adding to the discomfort of the surrounding passengers flying economy—Bones miraculously fulfilled his soothsaying mother-in-law's prophecy.

Chapter 25

Idioglossia

There's three of us on the sofa. Max and I are jammed up against the arm rests, and Bones is in the middle, taking up more than his share of third. The whole house smells of Brut for Men now. Bones is sitting tenderly on his sore arse, occasionally readjusting his posture, and grimacing at the pangs even the slightest movement induces. Max is wrapped up tight in his brown dressing gown, with a black beanie on his head and a blower heater at his feet. He's claiming to be in the firm grips of the flu. As far as I'm concerned, the selfish cunt should lock himself in his room until he gets over it, instead of spluttering black death all over the fucken house. But as the property is in his name by law, I have no option but to let it fly this time.

'What's with all the scratch marks on the floor?' Bones asks.

'Deceased estate,' Max says. 'Old man. Lived alone. His German Shepard started eating him not too long after he left the building. They had to put it down. Rules are you can't rehome them once they've had a taste of human flesh.'

Bones hasn't even told his folks he's back in Melbourne. Something along the lines of him not being ready to hear their outdated doctrine imposed upon his life choices. 'It's different times now,' he said. 'Those two useless fucks wouldn't even begin to understand how this life shit works now.'

We're all sitting watching that righteous ranga cunt mouth off on the television again, *The 7pm Saturday Review with Nigel Lassiter*.

'As a new father of a six-month-old, I am fearful of the kind of Australia my son will grow up in. Are we ourselves a child? Forced to leave the nursery door open so Big Ben or the White House can peek in and wipe our arse anytime they wish? Do we follow their house rules blindly? I vision a country where we stand up for what we believe in, where we take action to express our views outwards to the world. And if that upsets the north, then maybe it's time for us, as a country, as a people, to sever Britain's umbilical leash and spit out America's toxic teat.'

'Fuck this shit,' Bones says. 'Let's hit up The Duke and get on the piss.'

'Yeah, I'm keen,' I say. 'Sitting here watching this shit is fucken depressing me.'

'I'm feeling a bit rough, boys,' Max says, pulling his dressing gown tight and coughing phlegm into his fist. 'Think I'll sit this one out.'

'Come out, ya fucken selfish cunt,' Bones yells. 'I spent three years trapped in a freezing fucken cell, and you're choosing to spend your Saturday night on your fucken sofa?'

'Honestly, I feel exhausted, mate,' Max says. 'I'll come out next weekend, after pay day.'

'Walk up to the 7-Eleven, and shout yourself some Red

Bull and Tylenol,' Bones tells him.

'You two go out without me,' Max says. 'You don't need me there. I'll ruin the mood, anyway. Scare away all the ladies.'

'Two? Fuck that,' Bones says. 'Only takes the other to need a piss, then you're standing one-up on the side of the dancefloor looking like a fucken psychopath.'

'Call Trent, then,' Max offers.

'Nah, fuck him,' Bones says. 'Can't be arsed with him tonight. Spent enough time in close confines with cunts these last few years.'

Max coughs heavy, 'Shouldn't you not be drinking? With your infected arse.'

'Sort it out Monday,' Bones says. 'Get some antibiotics from one of those free doctors the government pays for. Get it cleared up before I check in with the folks so I don't have to cop all their judgemental parental shit.'

'Alright, Bones, looks like we're going two-up,' I say. 'I'll order us a ride, and we'll leave this lazy cunt here in peace to wank himself to sleep.'

****

Melbourne changes after dark. They leave that interesting fact out of the brochure. The torrent of tourists subsides, and all that's left is junkies on the footpath and network marketers sifting in the laneways—a long night ahead for both. Vandals creep out of their cracks too, spraying their clichéd stenciled statements all over other people's walls, where it will lie in wait until Monday morning to ram itself into the faces of the innocents walking to work. The police are out in force tonight as well. We pass through three roadside checkpoints on the ride to The Duke. Each time they stop our ride, ask us questions, and scan our driver licences. Keeping track of who's heading where with who.

'Enjoy the rest of your night, boys. Stay out of trouble.'

****

The line to The Duke is moving slowly. A pair of biceped bouncers at the door appear to be acting extra vigilant tonight. We get to the front of the line, and they give Bones a solid look up and down. His wardrobe has been limited to Minsk thrift stores these past few years, so I can understand why he's drawing a suspicious eye. His getup for this evening is scuffed green commando boots, white jeans, a white mesh singlet, and a leather jacket with large metal zips all over the place. I expect with his shaven head, bushman's beard, and his recent body transformation, he doesn't look too much like his licence photo anymore. One of the bouncers does a double take and ends up getting a second opinion from his mate before he finally waves us in.

The Duke of Westminster is one of our old haunts. Threw a bit of coin over this bar back in the day, that's for fair fucken certain. I can only pray that that coin was invested wisely on my behalf and will be returned to me one day with interest. The establishment is split into three levels. A pub on the ground level with Charlie Chaplins screaming at greyhounds; on the second level, a long bar with a small dancefloor; and at the very top of the stairs, a fancy rooftop bar that looks over Richmond Station and the tendrils of twisted metal that slither off towards the city skyline in the distance.

He's already waiting for us, Trent is. He's claimed a booth on the second floor, and he yells out at us before we have a chance to check out the rooftop.

'Fuck going up there, it's fucken freezing tonight. This here will be prime fucken real estate in two-hours' time,' he says as we slide into the booth. 'Trust me.'

As of now, the floor is essentially empty, bar a light scattering of sour faces getting slaughtered. The ones who had all the time in the world, until they didn't, and now they're angry. 'Disillusioned with dating,' they'll say, without understanding the mechanics of their words. Best to avoid. Mostly as a matter of principle. Trent tells us again that the rooftop will be shit, despite the fact I can hear the screams of girls spilling down the stairwell. I can only assume Trent started up there, some chick told him to fuck off, and he's retreated down to this desolate space with his tail between his legs. Trent always has this sixth sense of when we're doing something without him. He threw me a message on our way in. Asked me if there was anything going on tonight. And although his company repulses me, I felt an obligation to at least let him know where we're going, if not openly invite him. I'm not sure how long Bones will be sticking around town for, and with Max's enthusiasm to go out lukewarm at best, I need to keep Trent in the extended squad for the short term. At least until I find someone new and can fuck off all these cunts once and for all.

'So, what brings you back to Melbs?' Trent asks Bones. 'Thought you were done with us all? I remember you screaming that in my face at your leaving party.'

'Needed a bit of space from the missus and all that,' Bones says.

Trent smirks, 'That's why I'm not in a relationship. Value my own space too much.'

'Quite some company to keep all to yourself,' I say.

'Girls want independent guys, Jackson,' Trent bites. 'I'll write a fucken book on that paradox one day. Sign a copy for you. You'll pay full price for it, though, you fucken cheap cunt.'

'Tell Trent about your arse,' I tell Bones.

'I have a blocked pore. That was part of it too. Probably needs to see a doctor at some point.'

'Quit with the bullshit, mate,' Trent says. 'Max already messaged me the whole story. Karma for messing with God's design, if you ask me. If he wanted you buff, he would have built you that way from the start. No one to blame but yourself. At least I got a good laugh out of it, though. Cheers for that.'

As it's still quiet, I offer to buy the first round in anticipation of this bar eventually getting busier. You never want to be the one stuck lining up for the last round. Hinders all sorts of flow once girls enter the equation. Though, I'm certain this foresight is lost on Trent and Bones, and they most likely take my offer to buy the first round at its altruistic face value. And so, we down beers for a few hours, and it comes my turn to go up again, and again, and each time the line to get served gets longer, and all the other wasters lining up at the bar start to pretend not to see the other cunt who was clearly there before them. I've lost count of how many times I've been up now. Half a dozen at least. Could be more.

Trent's back up on his fucken soapbox.

'Girls claim they want a guy with a good sense of humour,' he says. 'They don't. What they mean by that, is some fuckhead who'll laugh at anything. I consider myself to have an incredibly distinguished sense of humour. You'll be lucky to hear a laugh out of me once every two years.'

'So, Bones. You reckon you'll end up paying her back?' I ask.

'Who? My mother-in-law?'

'Nah. The stripper.'

Bones shrugs, 'When we first started dating she told me a story. She'd do these private lap dances out the back of the club. Seedy rooms that stunk of wet dog and old leather. She had a regular. An old man with a crook back. Each time she sat his arthritis arse down on the sofa, she read him the house rules. Every client must empty their pockets before she danced. Claimed it was cos some Bulgarian dude went all stabby with a knife once. Anyway, Ol' Mate would put his wallet, phone, and keys down on the little ottoman next to the sofa. And they'd talk a bit. And he'd ask for a hug. And if he was drunk enough, or the night was late enough, he'd rest his head on her lap and drift off to sleep for a couple of minutes, dreaming of his dead wife. At least long enough for her to swipe a couple of notes from his wallet. Never so much he'd notice. After a year, it was enough to fund a holiday to Santorini. And she was laughing as she told me this story. She called him her, "angel investor." So, no. I don't feel guilty, if that's what you're asking. Beware the rules of the game you set.'

****

It's filled out now. Mostly with odds, ends, and all sorts. It's Trent's go for drinks. He's up at the bar chatting to these two identical twins. Both girls. He's holding our three bottles tight between his two hands, and I'm waving at him to hurry the fuck up because I'm fucken thirsty and the bottle in front of me is fucken empty. He tips his head towards us, and the two twins follow him over to our table carrying their two piss coffees that I'm certain Trent bankrolled. They're waif like, the identical twins, with long black hair down to their waist, and matching bright green dresses down to their ankles. Trent introduces us.

'This is Jackson. His missus gave him the arse a month back, so he's fucked in the head. And this is Bones, divorced with a kid in Russia.'

'I see you've met Trent,' I say to the twins. 'Never had a girlfriend. You, or you, could be his first.'

'Do you smell something?' one of the twins says to the other, twisting her nose.

'That'd be Bones's septic arse,' Trent says. 'Stabbed some roids in it. Got infected. Dick shrunk too.'

'So, what do you do?' I ask one of the twins, trying to get the conversation carriage back on track.

'Medicine,' she says.

She doesn't even ask me about myself. Just sips her piss coffee. Already fucken dead in the water, this one.

Thanks, Trent.

Cunt.

A moment.

'Who's keen for Chartreuse?' Trent asks the girls.

The twins exchange a butchery of indecipherable syllables between themselves, then turn back to us.

'Thanks, but we're going to go check out the rooftop.'

'Nice meeting you all,' says the other. 'Thanks for the drink—Sorry, I'm terrible with names.'

'Trent,' he says. 'Catch you later, maybe? Come back down if you get bored up there. You might get my number next time,' and he gives himself a sympathy laugh.

They walk away and up the stairs.

Trent's chin drops.

'Well, there goes some coin you'll never see again,' I say.

'Fucken hell, why'd you tell them I never had a girlfriend?'

'You fucken came out swinging at us,' I say.

'Yeah, but I was the one having a crack. So, what do you care?'

'How many times did you throw me under the bus back in the day, mate? Didn't realise there was one rule for you and one rule for the rest of us. If you want rules, fucken fine. But I'm sick of you making them up, as and when it suits you.'

'You're just jealous, Jackson,' Trent says.

'Of who? You? Please.'

'Of whoever a girl is talking to, who's not you.'

'Whatever. Tell yourself what you want to believe if that makes you feel better. Do what you have to do.'

'You probably didn't need to tell them about my arse, mate,' Bones says.

'What do you care?' Trent says. 'You already got a missus. Maybe concentrate on sorting out that mess first before you start signing up for more trouble.'

'And Chelsea didn't off me either,' I say. 'I don't know how you got that idea into your head.'

'Like shit she didn't, Jackson. Way too good for you that one was,' he says. 'We always said you were on borrowed time with her. What shocked us most, was it lasted as long as it did.'

I grab Trent by the hair and smash his face hard into the table. And when I pull his head back up his nose is bleeding bad, but I still don't let go of his hair. I readjust my grip and grab at him harder still.

'Look at me,' I say, his hair tight in my fist. 'Look at me, cunt.' And his eyes turn to look me right in my eye. 'Fucken

127

for once in your life, think about someone else other than yourself,' and I let go of his hair.

Blood streams from his nostrils.

'Always thinking about myself?' Trent says. 'Upstairs is pumping, full of girls, but we're hanging down on this shithole level here cos of that cunt there,' and he points to Bones.

'What do you mean because of me?' Bones asks.

'Your ex is upstairs, on the rooftop. Saw her as soon as I arrived up top, and I figured you wouldn't want to sit up there.'

'Which one?'

'I can't remember her name.'

'Where from?'

'Japan,' Trent says, his nose-blood cascading over his lips and dripping off his chin, and he's catching what he can of it in the palm of his hand.

'Who's she with?' Bones asks.

Trent shrugs his shoulders.

'Who the fuck is she with, Trent?'

'Some bloke.'

'Some bloke?' Bones says, rising to his feet.

'Mate, I wouldn't,' I tell Bones, but he's already thrown on his leather jacket and is storming for the stairs.

I follow behind.

'Wait, Bones. Wait!' But he's not listening.

No one ever fucken listens in this town.

Chapter 26
Pickled Pepper

We reach the top of the stairs, and Bones bursts out onto the rooftop, shoulders broad and swaying with menace. He's got the happy couple straight away. They're sitting on a pair of stools at the bar, legs entangled. She's wearing jeans and a white T-shirt, and her new bloke's wearing a purple floral long-sleeved shirt with the top three buttons undone, and he's tucked the mess into navy chinos which end in brown slip-on boots. Even though he's sitting down, his legs keep going, so I can tell there's some size to him for sure. Would have been a clear no-contest six years ago, but Bones is a beast now.

He walks up to them both.

'You're a piece of fucken work, aren't ya?' Bones says to her, then turns to her new bloke. 'Mate, let me give you some life advice. Run from this one. And when you're tired and out of breath, and you've got a stitch, and you taste blood in your mouth, take the deepest breath your lungs will allow, and run some more.'

'Who the fuck are you to tell me what to do, ya fuck?' the guy throws back at Bones. He turns to Bones's ex, 'This the one, is it?'

She nods.

'Controlling cunt, are we?' he spews at Bones, getting up off his stool to meet him at eye level.

'Too fucken right I tried to control her. Tried to control her holes from being ploughed by her boss at work drinks every Friday night.' And he turns to his ex, 'I know so much now. More than you ever knew I knew.'

Japan tugs at her new bloke's arm, asking him to sit down, but he shakes his head and shoves his palm in her face to tell her that it's okay, that he's got this.

'I'm gonna warn you, mate,' New Bloke says. 'Continuing to speak to her in this manner will be detrimental to the alignment of your jaw.'

'Used me for a fucken visa, she did,' Bones says.

'One more word, mate. I fucken dare ya.'

New Bloke's talking like someone who's spent a fair amount of time in fighting pyjamas, so I tug lightly on the arm of Bones's leather jacket.

'Let's go, mate,' I tell him. 'Fuck her. She's this dickhead's problem now.'

'Yeah. To fuck with the both of ya,' Bones says.

We walk away, back down the stairwell, and Bones stops on the flat between the floors and punches his hand hard at the wall.

'Fuck! FUCK!' he says.

The fingers of his right hand are in disorder and bleeding, and his pinkie hangs off ill, as if it's only the skin keeping it attached.

'You okay, mate?' I ask.

'Yeah,' he sighs. 'I'm fine.'

'Mate, fuck her. Bullet dodged, as far as I'm concerned. Let's head to the next bar.'

We stop by level two to pick up Trent, but the booth has been taken by others, so we continue down the stairs and out onto the street. It's coming on midnight, which is when Richmond really starts to pick up. The footpath is full of done-up girls, all looking beautiful, collecting on the ends of lines that are growing longer and longer with every passing minute. The traffic is dense and chaotic. Horns honk, and dangerous swerves by impatient cars occur at any moment a ride stops to drop off passengers. I want to calm Bones down and to not have this whole night go down the fucken gurgler when it's just getting started, so I nod my head at the kebab joint across the road.

'Keen for a halftime feed?'

'Yeah, alright.'

****

We're sitting on our stools at the window, unwrapping our kebabs from their foil, watching the hordes shuffle on by.

'Belarus isn't all bad,' Bones says. 'There's some nice parts, when you get out of town. We went on a holiday to this nice little lake once.'

Bones's right hand lies red and swollen at his side, so he's holding his kebab in his left hand, and as he takes his first bite his kebab shits itself; spraying lettuce, lamb juice, and chilli sauce all over his white jeans.

'Well, that's my fucken night done now, isn't it?' he says, slamming his mutilated kebab down on the bench.

And now I realise that I should have got Bones well away from here because across the road we see Japan and New Bloke walk out of The Duke. Bones's head bends to the side, and his shoulders twitch.

'Ignore them, mate,' I say. 'Not worth the trouble.'

Their ride pulls up and New Bloke opens the door for her like a true fucken gentleman. The cunt even bows his head and does a roll of his hand like some fucken Victorian butler, and Bones is up off his stool and striding across the road. In a camel's blink, he's up on the boot of their ride, banging on the back window with his one good fist.

'Had her in her prime, I did!' Bones yells. 'Enjoy my scraps, cunt.'

Every hem and collar in the line for The Duke turns and looks, so I run up behind Bones and tug on the back of his jacket, trying to get him down off the boot before the bouncers or some passing cops get too interested in his impromptu street performance.

'C'mon, mate. I know, I know,' I say.

Unmovable.

'Enjoy her fucken moustache, mate,' Bones says.

And New Bloke has had enough. He opens his ride door, and it's instantly collected by a passing car. Bang. The door is sent aerial, a flying circular saw, hurtling through the air, out of sight, down the street. Gone. I hear a metallic scrape and a gasp from the audience walking the street. And now, a still silence. An awful still silence. And I know it's coming. I fucken know it is.

'Ambulance! Someone call a fucken ambulance!' some guy screams from down the street.

I walk over to the crowd encircling the scene and push between the concerned parties. There's a guy on his knees cradling his girlfriend's head in his hands.

'No, no, no,' he keeps saying over and over as red and white slop falls from her neck, spilling onto the lap of his stone chinos. Her body lies five metres away, twitching. I turn back to check on Bones, but he's gone from where he was, so I walk away before any burden of the scene has a chance to tether itself to me for good.

****

Sirens, sirens.

Flashing lights of cop cars speed past me on my short walk to Richmond Station, followed hotly by an overly ambitious ambulance.

I arrive on the platform just as my train pulls away, and there's a near thirty-fucken-minute wait until the next one. Once again, I am alone, the sole occupant of the platform. The very last thing I need tonight is time with my own thoughts. Another level of hell, that is.

I feel a piss coming on, but they've shut all the toilets at the station because of all the junkies who consider the shitters a nice place to spend the night. Faced once more with the genuine prospect of pissing my pants, I walk over to the edge of the track—mind the gap. As I reach to unzip, I spot a poster promoting that cunt Nigel Lassiter's new late-night radio show, *Pillow Talk*. His smiling, smug face is at me, so I walk over and whip out my dick and start pissing YOU CUNT in cursive across his face, but before I get to the 'C', I sense a figure standing behind me. I strangle my stream and look over my shoulder. There's a wintery mist that surrounds the station, that sort you only get very late at night, the first forming of an early dew. It makes it hard to figure out who the figure is at first. But the mist soon offers a moment of transparency, enough that I can tell it's not a cop. And it's not one of those platform prefects either. As the mist rolls across the station and dissipates through the wire fence into the back streets filled with old brick buildings, I see it's just a sole commuter. Some bloke who, like myself, has most likely dealt with enough shit for one night already. I tuck my dick back into my pants as a common courtesy to the one-man crowd and take a seat on the cold wooden bench, my bladder now emptied enough that I should get back to Max's joint without incident.

He's standing about twenty-feet away, this guy is, on the edge of the platform, but he keeps looking over at me. And it's only when I hold my stare back at him, to assure him that I'm ready to fucken stomp his teeth out if he wants to have a go, that I realise I know him.

'Jackson?' he calls out.

It's Stefano. He worked with Chelsea at the florist. A slightly flamboyant dude, mid-twenties. Bit of chub on him, but he's somehow managed to stuff himself into a pair of skinny jeans.

'Hey mate,' I say, and he walks over to me.

'You been alright?' he asks, taking a seat on the bench.

'Yeah, good, mate. You?'

'Good.'

'Good.'

'Chelsea told me you two parted ways,' he says. 'Sorry things didn't work out.'

'It's alright. I'm enjoying being single, actually.'

'Yeah, well, the novelty of that will wear off one day.'

He gives off a half laugh, sighs, then stares off down the tracks and winces.

'How's she doing, anyway?' I ask.

'No idea. Haven't kept in touch. She handed in her resignation soon after you guys—Went your separate ways.'

'Did you notice her acting weird or anything? Not herself?'

'Maybe. Hard to tell what's really going on in someone's head sometimes.'

'Thing is, the end came all a bit sudden. I just have a whole lot of loose ends that I'm trying to tie up, you know?'

'Yeah, I know.'

'Fair few fucken gaps in her story, that's for certain.'

'Look, Jackson. I'm only going to tell you this because I've been where you've been before. More than once, to be honest. A few months back at work, I took a phone order for a big bouquet of flowers. Now, when we take a phone order, we fill in a card on behalf of the giver. Usual procedure: who's it from, who's it to, what you want to say, all that fucken garbage. So, I'm on the phone to this guy, got my pen in hand, and I ask him who the flowers are for. And he says, "Chelsea." I think nothing of it at that point, plenty of Chelsea in this world. Then, I ask him what he wanted his message to say. He goes, "Follow your heart." So, I write it down. And then I ask him for the delivery address, and he says, "It's for Chelsea. The Chelsea you work with." I thought it was a bit weird at the time, him not being you, but then I figured that it could be a relative or something, or even one of our creepy customers. You run into a decent number of nutcases working at a florist, that's for sure. Anyway, she seemed flustered at first, when I handed her the flowers, but she smiled when she read the card, and she told me that it was just a friend. I guess I gave her a slightly disapproving look, cos she got all moody and goes to me, "You either trust me or you don't." And I just left it at that.'

A train arrives with a violent shattering of the tracks and a slamming of air brakes. It's Stefano's train, not mine.

'Well, this is me,' he says stepping onto his train. 'Take it easy, mate.'

'Wait, Stefano. Who was it from? The name on the card?'

The train doors start to beep.

'It won't matter. Not in the grand scheme of things.'

'Please! Just the name.'

The doors begin to close in on him. Through the last inch of gap, before the train carries him off into the cold misty darkness, he tells me.

'Peter.'

Peter

Chapter 27

Painted Whores

Monday.

Life goes on.

Rick's back from Bali, his saggy arse planted firmly on the corner of Dita's desk as he gives the Indonesians a good spray.

'Got to be careful in Bali, Dita. They like to fuck over tourists. Smell your wallet coming a mile away. You got to learn to haggle cos there's one price for locals and one price for tourists. Fucken racists. So, I ask one of 'em for a quote for an hour-long massage, and she tells me five dollars. Fucken house deposit where they're from. So, I tell her, "Get fucked. Two bucks or I'm walking away." Called her bluff. She takes my two bucks and gets on with the job. Got to keep a close eye on these third world cunts. They'll take you for all your worth if you're not careful. The masseuse had a lovely figure, though, much like yourself.'

Earlier this morning, Bones woke up on the sofa in full fever. He looked all hot and sweaty, but he kept mouthing off about how fucken cold Max's house was. At first, Max and I thought it was just a bad hangover because he threw up six or seven times in the shitter yesterday afternoon. But he went downhill fast in the evening. Passed out for a bit and started mouthing off in his sleep. Something about not being hungry. So, this morning, we had no choice but to phone it in to the doctors. Max called in sick to work, and we carried a delirious Bones down the rickety front steps and chucked him across the back seat of Max's car. Then Max ran him down to the medical centre at the local shopping plaza for a check-up.

Dita slides her chair over to my desk.

'Good weekend, Jackson?'

'Yeah, it was alright.'

'Do much?'

'Just caught up with some mates. You?'

'I checked out that Picasso exhibit at the NGV.'

'Oh yeah, I've seen that advertised on trams. Any good?'

'Yeah, top shelf. It gets you thinking, doesn't it? Art. There was this one painting, *Le Moulin de la Galette*,' Dita says in perfect French. 'It was a picture of guys and girls hanging out in this Paris bar. Post-impressionist, before he went all angles. Anyway, the caption beside the painting said that it reflected Picasso's growing obsession with this bar, "where patrons and prostitutes rub shoulders."'

'Sounds cool.'

'Do you not think it was assuming of the curator to call the girls at the bar, "prostitutes"? I mean, maybe she was right. I'm not completely versed in the history of the time. But—'

'Maybe they were just out for a drink?'

'Yes, Jackson. That's exactly what I was thinking. Maybe they were just out for a drink.'

And her eyes drift off and look out the window in what I first take as contemplation, but when I follow her gaze I see two abseiling window washers mopping the outside glass with squeegee brushes.

'Anyway,' she says, 'it got me thinking about a lot of stuff.'

'How this town cast fuck all of your lot in bronze?'

'About how quickly everyone lost sight of the ladder.'

****

Wednesday. Hump day. Turns out Bones's arse was way worse than he thought. Too much for the doctors at the shopping plaza medical centre to handle, so they had to phone triple zero and order him a ride in an ambulance. The big guns at the Royal Melbourne Hospital diagnosed him with a glute abscess and threw him straight into emergency surgery. Scalpeled open his arse and drained two pints of pus. Thing is, they can't stitch it up like a normal wound because it could get infected, and he might end up with septicaemia and lose a leg or even potentially his dick and sack if the infection were to spread. So, they had to leave the wound open. Six inches long and one inch deep. Three months to heal, they said. That's if there are no secondary complications. So, Bones had no other option. Had to phone it in to his folks. Now he's back in his childhood bedroom, confined to his single bed, getting the gaping hole in his arse cleansed daily by his mother. The dressing changed, and the wound re-packed with sterile gauze to absorb the tissue exudate. And his wall punch at The Duke ended up breaking his right hand in three places, so that's in full cast for the foreseeable future.

Poor cunt.

What a fucken nightmare.

****

It's just before lunchtime, and Dita is over at my desk again. My boss is making himself another shake of some shit in the kitchen, and he frowns his overgrown eyebrows at us as he walks back to his office. I smile at him and lean back in my chair. Dita doesn't notice this exchange, or if she does, doesn't react to it.

'What's on for the weekend, Jackson?' she asks.

'Catching up with mates. You?'

'No plans yet,' and she leans into me and speaks softly. 'My boyfriend's away on business.'

And now she's got me thinking. How many stories started this way? Two partners who justified their betrayal by making an original partner nothing more than a comical footnote in their meeting story. Words like 'fate' and 'destiny' and phrases like 'written in the stars.' And they sell the whole sordid scenario as some fucken meet-cute to family and friends. Nothing ever occurs from two cold starts. There's always collateral. I remember Freud mouthing off about something similar in some book they made us read back in primary school. The injured third party. And fuck me, I don't know her boyfriend, but I'd know he'd do the same to me if given the opportunity. Without a shred of doubt, without even having to think about it, I know he'd do the same to me. Fuck him. He's probably balls deep in network marketers while he's away on business anyway, so it's all fucken karma, as far as I'm concerned. And it'll be a funny story we'll tell our friends and a romantic story we'll tell our kids. Always follow your heart, we'll justify. Do what you feel is right. When you know, you know. Fuck him, I say, fuck him.

'Yeah? You should come out with me and my mates,' I say.

'They won't mind me cramping their style?'

'I can't foresee that being an issue, no.'

'Where are you thinking of heading?'

'Southbank, probably.'

'Could be keen. Should we invite Will too?' she asks, looking over at him. He can't hear us. A large pair of headphones have recently become a permanent fixture on his head.

'Will doesn't drink anymore,' I tell her. 'He had a bit of a blowout a few Fridays back. Couldn't handle his piss. Got nude. Rather embarrassing for all concerned. Probably best not to push the cause. He's a bit sensitive about the subject.'

****

I'm taking my afternoon slash at the urinal, and my boss rocks up next to me and starts with the small talk before his weak stream finally gets going.

'Ah, hump day nearly done and dusted,' he says.

'Yep. Two sleeps till Friday,' I say. 'Much on for the weekend?'

'Nah, quiet one for me, mate. Just taking it easy. Maybe a gym session or two. A few laps of the Tan. What about you?'

'Heading out on town with Dita.'

I zip up, chuck my hands under a token spout of water, grab violently at the paper cloth dispenser, and let the men's room door bang heavy behind me. I sit back down at my desk and take a deep sigh because, like every lawmaker in history, I am being forced to write out what should—by all rights—be fucken givens. I'm pretty certain Moses was just a bloke who didn't want his mates to root his missus, and he packed a whole lot of other stuff around it to smooth off the edges. I guess some cunts just need the boundaries spelt out to them. I start with the title, *The Act of Mateship*. I'll be working late tonight.

Chapter 28

The Ladder

It's Friday morning, coming on eleven. My boss has had Dita in his office for over an hour. I'm close to phoning the cunt in to the cops for indentured servitude. Finally, his door opens. He thanks Dita for her time and calls me into his office with a chest beating bravado that annoys me now as much as it must have done his estranged wife. I'm starting to see more and more why Audrey chose to have her uterus chewed on by her personal trainer's parasitic sperm, save hearing another round of sterile shit fall from my boss's mouth at the day-end dinner table. I get up from my desk and walk towards his office. The possible reasons for his request for my audience run through my mind. My premium forecasts are too low, a client has complained that I didn't action their request in a timely manner, or he's crying himself to sleep each night, pining for someone somewhere to give two fucks he exists, and he's just after some advice from another guy on how to make the pain stop hurting.

'Yeah, close the door behind you, mate,' he says.

And I take a seat.

'I've been meaning to ask you,' he says. 'How'd your sessions go?'

'Good, good. Talked some stuff through.'

'I'm glad you took something from it. Look, Jackson, I want to be open and honest with you. The team leader role, well, Sydney has gazed into their crystal ball, and they're forecasting a potential contraction of the Melbourne market next quarter. Long story short, they've decided to delay replacing the team leader position for the foreseeable future.'

I lean forward in my seat, 'Really?'

'But here's the good news: A senior account manager has just jumped ship in Sydney, and they asked me if anyone down here would be interested in an internal transfer. They need someone who can hit the ground running, who knows Destiny. So, I put your name forward.'

'To move to Sydney?'

'Yes, but they're willing to offer you a generous relocation package.'

'How much?'

'25K to get you set up in Sydney. And a healthy raise too.'

'25K upfront?'

'Well, I think the way it works is you get to Sydney first, then you lodge an expense claim. But essentially, yes, upfront. Now, I know this is something that you might want to take some time to consider. Sydney—they understand that too. But, at the same time, there is some sense of urgency on their part to fill the position as soon as possible. Thoughts?'

'I'd have to have a think about it. Got a bit going on here, to be honest.'

'As your boss, Jackson, I'd hate to see you go. But as your mate, I think this would be a great move for your career. Senior would look good on your CV.'

'When do I have to make a decision by?'

'Think about it over the weekend, and let's touch base early next week.'

This will suit my boss fine, the creepy fuck. Run the one bloke in his mind standing between him and Dita, out of town for fucken ever. And I feel like doing it right now, right here in this office. Feel like calling him on it. Feel like telling him to his face that I know what he is. That I'm ten steps ahead of this sad sack-of-shit at all times, and, quite frankly, I'm insulted the condescending fuck feels he can play me as easily as he thinks he can. But he doesn't deserve that. Doesn't deserve the benefit of my insight. So, I withhold that courtesy, and I thank him for thinking of me, and I tell him that I will give serious thought to the opportunity and will let him know my decision once I've consulted those closest to me.

I rise from my seat.

'And while I have you here, Jackson,' he says.

'Yep,' and I sit back down.

'I know you're helping Dita settle in, and I appreciate your dedication to helping her get up to speed with Destiny. But make sure your August numbers are your first priority. If she has any questions, I've told her to come to me in the first instance from now on.'

'Okay (Cunt).'

I sit back down at my desk, and I'm fucking fuming. I look over to Dita who is staring straight at her computer screen like she's had a pair of fucken blinkers sewn on. And I'm filled with a burning hatred and disgust at my boss, and any last remnant of sympathy I once had for the cunt has gone. Stewing in his empty, soulless existence, he's grasping at the only structure that places him ahead of anyone anywhere in this fucken messed up world. Ruthlessly asserting his pseudo-authority by unsaid threat of cancelled pay. Spreading the isolation that has found him in his furnished apartment like a plague across the office. Sitting alone, working alone, I feel the pressure of the day rise, and I start to look at the frosted doors with the company logo, and I start to picture myself slowly getting up, walking calmly through them, pressing G in the lift, and never coming back. And all the resulting confusion and mayhem as my cunt of a boss has to work out where I went and if I'm coming back and if I'm even alive, and when Sydney asks whether I've accepted the job offer or not, he has to tell them he doesn't know because he doesn't know where I am, and he tries to phone me, but I've changed my number, and my clients start complaining that I'm not replying to their messages in a timely manner, and the cunt doesn't even know where I live now, and I seep into the city never to be seen or heard of by him again. But here is the truth of the matter— because it's important to be honest with yourself in situations like this—: With my current financial circumstance, I wouldn't get much further than Max's couch. And there I would lie: single, poor, and now unemployed. And all it takes is a moment of thought to realise you don't have as many options as you truly wish you did. She said our twenties were for living, that we only get them once, and our thirties would be for saving and settling down. So, after six-years of being dragged along with that fucked up doctrine, there's fuck all in my bank account right now. Though, at least I managed to keep my neck out of the red, which is more than she can say. Hence the whole importance of that team leader promotion that was supposed to be mine. And so, for the remainder of the afternoon, I have no choice but to generate forecast graphs and tweak slide presentations. Pick up the phone, make my calls. I book three face-to-face meetings next week and one for the week after. And I'm carrying on cold calling cunts until I can take it no longer, and I headbutt my keyboard. Dita looks over. It's the first time she has since she left my boss's office. I smile back and shrug. She returns my smile, but her big blue eyes don't smile like they normally do. And as I mop my blood off my keyboard with my multi-purpose wipes, the skyscrapers outside the windows begin to rise. They get taller, and they stand over me, and the cranes start to look down on me, and the sky gets further and further away, and the walls of the office close in on me, and I can't breathe. The walls aren't real. The walls aren't real. The walls aren't real. And I see the doors, and I want to run, but I know I can't because I won't get far.

25K.

Chapter 29
The Mask of Middle Class

F ucken sign it,' I say. 'Fucken sign it or you're not coming out with us tomorrow night. I made Max sign it, Bones will sign it when his arse is fixed, and you're gonna fucken sign it now too.'

I headed here straight after work. Told Trent I wanted to talk. Clear the air. As soon as he opened his door, I burst straight in and slammed it down on his kitchenette counter. I'm holding a pen out at the cunt. Trent's nose has a bandage across the bridge, and it looks slightly off centre to my eye. He should look at getting it professionally reset before it causes him too much sinus trouble. Still, when you run your tongue like he did, you have to be prepared to suffer the consequences of your words. At least now, his nose distracts the eye from his ears. The cunt can at least thank me for that.

'This is a fucken joke, this is,' Trent says.

'Read it, understand it, sign it,' I say. 'We need some sort of order to all this.'

'Fucken hell.'

Trent grabs the pen from my hand and hovers it over the last page of The Act of Mateship.

His apartment is a disgrace at present. I'm starting to realise he must have cleaned up for us when we were last over. There's a pile of pizza boxes stacked on the stove top, and a whole lot of empty Coke bottles thrown next to a rubbish bin that's spilling over its sides.

'You've lost your fucken mind, Jackson,' Trent says.

'Look, mate. You wanna be forty, in a bar, and you offer to buy a chick a shot of Chartreuse, and she goes to you, "Fuck off, Grandpa."'

Trent's chin drops to his chest, and I put my hand on his shoulder. I speak to him softer.

'Because that's where we're heading, mate. We're all staring down the Great Dry. All of us. That's why things have got to change. They have to. Read it. Understand it. Sign it.'

And with pen in hand, Trent scribbles his name, date, and signature.

Chapter 30

The Act of Mateship

1) The Pursuit of Company Fair Play

The following is to provide teammates a guide to fair play in the pursuit of companionship in order to promote *mateship*. An honest attempt to assist fellow mates to meet a companion must be made at all times. Therefore, the following is prohibited under any circumstances:

a) If a fellow teammate is conversing with a companion sitting next to him, at no point is another teammate allowed to place himself on the other side of the companion in question and participate in the aforementioned conversation. The offence is considered offside and may be called out by the teammate that has been infringed upon. If it is essential that the offender subsequently requires a seat, he must discreetly retire from his illegal position and sit himself on the furthest flank of his fellow teammate [in relation to the companion] and any conversation from then on entered into, must be made only in assistance of his fellow teammate's pursuit. Sitting directly across the table from a companion is also considered offside.

b) If a fellow teammate declares that he and his companion are going for a 'cigarette outside', a 'Chartreuse shot at the bar', or any other similar vacation from the team, no teammate(s) shall vocalise their desire to come. A declaration of leave signifies a positive progression in conversation, therefore the teammate is within his rights to be given a degree of privacy for up to, but not exceeding, thirty minutes.

c) Team law, in the interest of *mateship*, expressively forbids a teammate from requesting his fellow teammate's companion for a dance. The aforementioned act is considered unfair play and is a threat to the pursuit of companionship. Just because one teammate is full enough to move to music, doesn't mean a fellow teammate should be forced to do so under duress. Additionally, twirling a teammate's companion on the dancefloor is considered an automatic blatant breach of the Act of Mateship. Refer [Act 5 (b)].

d) Excessive alcohol drinking is condoned. However, it is each teammate's individual responsibility to manage their alcohol intake so that it does not conversely affect the collective team's performance in the pursuit of companionship. Therefore, a 'three strikes, ride home' policy applies. Strikable offences include:

(i) Deliberate flatulence.

(ii) Singular use of the word 'cunt.'

(iii) Multiple use of the word 'fuck.' Defined as three or more.

(iv) Arguing with a teammate's companion from a position of perceived academic authority.

(iv) Appearing in any physical or mental state which motivates anyone (companion or otherwise) to ask, 'Is your mate okay?'

2) Classification of Companion

The following laws should apply:

A companion shall automatically become a Sourced Potential Companion if a teammate has taken action to source and engage the companion himself. This may be within the bar or party environment or it may involve a previously known person who has formally agreed to meet a teammate. The Act of Mateship shall henceforth know these companions classed under this clause as SPC or Sourced Potential Companion.

Please Note: fellow teammates are prevented at all times from pursuing an SPC.

If an SPC arrives with friends, these single associates are considered approachable under The Pursuit of Company Fair Play. If a teammate without an assigned SPC applies conversation to a single associate for a period lasting no shorter than ten minutes, the status of the single associate is automatically upgraded to Assisted Potential Companion or APC.

Unlike an SPC, a teammate is only entitled to temporary exclusivity in pursuit of an APC. This is a period of one hour, commencing immediately from the promotion of the single associate to APC. If something of significance happens within that hour, such as an exclusive relocation of the pairing within the bar or party environment, or a kiss, then the APC is promoted to the status of SPC for the remainder of the evening, and a permanent suspension of pursuit is applied to all other teammates. However, if nothing of significance happens within that one-hour period after the APC status is declared, their title is automatically revoked, and they return to their original classification of single associate. Therefore, they are once again considered approachable by all participating teammates. Refer [Act 2 (b)]. This code is employed not only to give fellow teammates a fair chance but also to prevent teammates flogging dead horses.

3) Mateship Protection

Mateship shall exist only between members of the predetermined party. Civil pleasantries towards others are tolerated within reason, but any unwarranted invitation to other male(s) to join our designated drinking area is highly prohibited. There is one rare exception to Mateship Protection:

a) Mateship Protection is void should the invitation of the male person(s) have reasonable potential to introduce significant company which would far outweigh the negative effects of the original male invitee(s).

Case Study: While waiting at the bar, a guy called Daniel from Brisbane engages you in conversation about how useless the bartender is and how long you have to wait in line for a drink when all you want is a beer. He's taller and better looking than you. While at first you assume he is in pursuit of company like yourself, he goes on to reveal that he's flown down to Melbourne with his girlfriend to visit his sister, and he points to a table where you see his girlfriend, his sister, and all his sister's friends seated. In this scenario, it is perfectly appropriate to invite him as a temporary member of the team, under guise of friendship, knowing full well that at some point later in the evening you will be introduced to his sister and her single associates.

Please Note: it is imperative that on returning to the table, this back story is immediately communicated to all members of the team to assure them that no breach of Mateship Protection has taken place.

4) Venue Choice

Venue choice shall be decided by democratic vote unless either of the following two circumstances apply:

(a) An SPC *gives* a precise and specific invitation to a teammate, including both a time and a venue.

(b) An SPC *accepts* a precise and specific invitation from a teammate, including both a time and a venue.

Upon arriving at the venue at the specified time, the group will allow for a window of up to one hour for the SPC to arrive. Should the SPC not arrive within the hour window, the democratic vote of venue choice reapplies. However, if the SPC does arrive within the window, the sourcer of the SPC has dictatorial control of venue choice for the remainder of the evening.

Please Note: in the rare occurrence that two or more team members simultaneously claim venue choice under either [Act

4 (a)] or [Act 4 (b)], or in any scenario in which democratic voting is deadlocked, then venue choice is decided by the winner of the drinking game *Fingers.*

5) Prosecution
Offences fall into two categories:

a) Minor Drunken Misdemeanour
As mentioned in [Act 1 (d)], this falls under the 'three strikes, ride home' policy, and eviction from the evening is considered a just and sufficient punishment.

b) Blatant Breach of the Act of Mateship
If you feel another teammate has blatantly breached The Act of Mateship, you must put your accusation in written message within twenty-four hours of the incident occurring, ensuring all teammates who were present are included in the communication. The accused teammate has the following two courses of action:

> (i) Plead guilty and receive an instant two-week suspension from weekend pursuits.

> (ii) Plead not-guilty and face a four-week suspension from weekend pursuits if found guilty.

If the teammate pleads not-guilty, the accusation goes to a democratic voting process in which the determination of conviction or non-conviction is decided by the majority vote of all members present on the night of the incident. If the voting is hung, the member is declared not-guilty.

Please sign as confirmation that you have read and understood
The Act of Mateship.

Name:
Date:
Signature:

Chapter 31

Divine Rose

We're at Troubadours, Saturday night, parked up on the front deck overlooking the Yarra River. The heat lamp next to us offers warmth. I'm sitting at a table with Max and Trent, and Dita's yet to rock up. The lights of Southbank Promenade spill onto the swollen river revealing a swirling diarrhoea brown. I wouldn't be surprised if the raised water level was caused by the literal shit of every fucken arsehole in this city, but Max assures me it's from sediment released by the heavy rains, and perhaps a few kangaroo and koala carcasses from farms upstream. I count nine police choppers in the sky, hovering high above the tops of skyscrapers, obliterating shadows with their searchlights.

The sparsely littered clientele at Troubadours is tolerable, in part due to the casino downstream that tends to mop up both poles of societal filth that frequent this part of town.

'Jesus Christ, Jackson,' Trent says, getting up off his stool. 'Why do you always choose shit bars like this? There's only one hot chick here, and she's stuck behind the fucken bar. Let's fuck off this joint and go to Psychopomp.'

'Sit down and drink your beer,' I say. 'There's no fucken way we're going to Psychopomp. Dita's on her way, and I've got the full fucken hour for her to arrive, by right. And either way, we're not going to Psychopomp.'

A navy inflatable, with a machine gun turret upfront, charges upstream towards the MCG. Its bow bounces against the dirty current, spawning wakes of brown sludge that crash against the concrete riverbank. It's more dangerous than it looks, the Yarra. A couple of years back, two Welsh backpackers tried to swim across it to impress some Colombian chicks. They didn't even make it to halfway before the river swallowed them whole. Cops fished them out from under a pontoon three months later.

'Anyone checked in on Bones?' Max asks.

'Nah, fuck it,' Trent says. 'He's his folk's problem now.'

'I'm sure he'll let us know when his arse is fixed,' I say.

'So, with this bro codes thing?' Trent asks. 'This chick from your work rocks up, and you've got one hour to get into her? Then, when nothing happens, I'm free to have a crack?'

'Fucken no, Trent. Jesus Christ. You can read, can't you?'

'Yeah, well, you're good at making simple things complicated.'

'Okay, I'll explain this to you one last fucken final time. I invited her. That makes her a Sourced Potential Companion. An SPC. She's off the table for both you and Max, full stop, for fucken ever. Got it? If she brings a friend, then her friend would be classified as an Assisted Potential Companion. An APC. In which case, you, or Max, could engage her in small pleasantries with the potential of seeing her again at some point in the future. Got it?'

'She's bringing a friend, is she?' Max asks all excited.

'Possible,' I say. 'Doubtful, though.'

****

Our beers are empty. It's Trent's round, but he refuses to go to the bar, much to the utter disgust of Max and myself. It's all because behind the bar, a petite blond bartender is violently thrashing a cocktail shaker with six cocktail glasses lined up in front of her. Our beers are empty, we're thirsty, and there's some tall nerdy bartender bloke with thick-rimmed glasses standing behind the bar with his fucken hands in his pockets, but still Trent refuses to go and get his round, dare he risk being served by him instead of her. I follow his eyes, fixated on each pour of the shaker, the tearing of mint leaves, the final addition of straws, the handing over of the credit card, and when the receipt is torn from the terminal, Trent leaps up from his seat and runs to the bar. The nerdy bartender bloke greets Trent with a big smile, but Trent blanks him and throws his order at the blonde. He leans up hard against the bar, his groin riding its curvature as she pops open our three beers. He points over to us, and she leans towards him, and there's a brief exchange of conversation. Trent returns, finally, with our three beers and a smug smile on his face.

'Hot bartender's into me,' he says.

'Why? What she say?' Max asks.

'Smiled. Wanted to know my plans for the evening.'

'That's customer service, mate,' I tell him. 'Best learn not to confuse the two.'

****

She's here, finally, Dita is. She's wearing a slim pink dress and this fluffy red shoal thing. She pulls up a bar stool next to me, apologises for running late, and I introduce everyone to each other.

'How's your night been so far?' Dita asks the table.

158

'Okay,' says Trent.

'Good,' says Max.

'So, what do you guys do?' she goes.

'Computers.'

'Teach.'

'Nice,' she says. 'Well, I'm going to get a drink. Would anyone like anything?'

'Nope.'

'Nah.'

'Thanks, Dita,' I say. 'We're in a round, but thanks for the offer.'

Dita gets up and heads over towards the bar, and I lean into the table.

'Fucken hell, guys. Would it hurt to contribute something to the conversation? Pretend you're fucken normal for once?'

'What's the point?' Trent goes. 'Can't have a crack. Wasted words.'

'Can't keep track of all your rules,' Max says. 'Figure it best to shut up.'

'Jesus Christ. You can still talk. Just don't swear, don't say weird shit, and don't chuck me under the fucken bus. It's as simple as that.'

'Yeah, but as I said,' Trent says, his eyes looking sideways at the blond bartender serving Dita, 'wasted words for me, isn't it?'

****

The blond bartender has joined us now. She's on her break and parked up on a stool next to Trent. He lights her up a cigarette and one for himself too. And now Trent won't shut the fuck up. He's getting all existential on Blondie Bartender.

Telling her that if he had his time over again, he'd choose to come back as a parrot.

'Because of all the bright pretty colours?' she teases.

'No!' Trent snaps. 'It's got fuck all to do with all their bright pretty colours.'

I can tell Dita finds the whole situation somewhat confusing. She asks me, as an aside, how I know these guys.

'Mates from school,' I tell her.

As for Max, he just keeps staring down the neck of his beer in silence. Blondie Bartender stubs out her cigarette and returns to the bar, and Trent gives himself a congratulatory nod in acknowledgement of his perceived groundwork. Then he gets all loud and excited.

'Cheers, everyone! To tonight!' he says.

And our green bottles meet with Dita's tall glass for obligatory clinks in the middle of the table.

****

Trent keeps looking over to the bar. The tall nerdy fuck with the thick-rimmed glasses is chasing Blondie Bartender behind the bar, playfully slapping her with his yellow bar cloth, and spraying her with a bottle of green disinfectant. She's giggling and Trent's squirming in his chair. Nerdy Fuck wraps Blondie Bartender up in a big bear hug from behind and kisses her on the cheek. Trent snarls. Literally. Exposed incisors. And he's up off his stool and storming up to the bar.

'Go on,' he yells at her. 'Keep chasing the tall, dark, and handsome, you superficial sack-of-shit. I promise you: one day you'll be me and I'll be you.'

Blondie Bartender and Nerdy Fuck, still in embrace, stare at Trent, stunned, as he storms back to our table, his heels scuffing the ground.

'Fuck this shithole,' Trent says. 'I'm going to Psychopomp. You cunts coming?'

'No way,' I say. 'No chance.'

Max gets up off his stool and picks up his coat.

'Really?' I ask.

'Got chatting to a chick last time I was there. Waiting in line for the shitters. She ended up taking me home.'

'Sounds like a bullshit story to me,' Trent says.

'Swear to God,' Max says.

'Well, how come I never met her, then?' Trent asks.

'Next morning, I asked her if she'd like to do dinner sometime. Find a nice restaurant. She got all angry, accusing me of being presumptuous. Never heard from her again.'

'That's a "tree fell in a forest" root,' Trent says. 'If it did happen, it's as good as if it didn't.'

Dita goes to me, 'You know, I think I'm about ready to call it a night, so you can go with them if you want to.'

'Nah, it's okay. There's no way I'm going to Psychopomp.'

'Right, Max. Let's fuck off this lot, then,' Trent says. 'And as for your rules, Jackson. Fuck you, ya fucken faggot. As if two weeks banned from your company is any form of punishment whatsoever. You come back to us after your missus finally grew the balls to chuck you in, and you think you're better than us? Always thought you were a cunt. Old, weird, and single. No fucken rules gonna stop where you're heading, mate.'

You will know who he is

Peter

Come on, you fucken idiot

You know how these things work

161

Chapter 32

Drag Innit (Lousy Plumber)

Our ride is stuck in traffic on Queen Street. A couple of cars in front of us, a truck is trucking in a crane that will build a new skyscraper, taller than the tallest one they built last year. On the footpath outside a 7-Eleven, a disturbed fat chick is pacing circles. She lifts her black dress over her large saggy tits, bends over, and spurts indefinable yellow liquid across the footpath. Consistency would suggest shit, however volume leans towards piss.

'Merry Christmas, Your Majesty!' she screams at nobody.

Dita's barrel left and I'm barrel right. Her apartment is not really on my way, as the crow flies, but the detour is small enough that it keeps it in the confines of common sense. Someone normal to share some time with at least. You learn to savour sane company when you hang out with my lot. The driver has his radio set to Nigel Lassiter's new late-night radio show, *Pillow Talk*.

'Are you going to let this police state suck the art out of your life. If you don't have expression, what do you have? A nameless grave. Yes, your grave may have letters, and those letters will form words, but your name, *your* name, will mean nothing. An empty utterance of vacuous meaning. First, they put eyes on every corner, and now they want to put ears in every pocket? With no liberty, how do you stand apart from all those that have gone before? Next Saturday on Swanston Street, we come together as one. Next Saturday on Swanston Street, we show all of Australia how loud our one voice—'

'Your radio come with other stations, mate?' I ask the driver.

He bashes a button on the dash and fills the ride with INXS.

'Mediate'

Do you miss her?

Who?

You know

Not in the sense most would think

What does it feel like to you?

It's not nice

Describe it

It's hard to put into words

Is it more a sadness or an anger?

Closer to anger

Maybe beyond anger

This rage you can't throw

Suffocate

Hate

The person closest to you, gifting you hell

It's the not knowing

It's the not knowing that's the worst

I'd rather cop a boot to the teeth any day of the week

But do you believe she intended to hurt you?

I wouldn't have done that to her
I wouldn't have made her feel this way
Never in a million years
Never
Wouldn't be able to live with myself
How can you be so certain of that?
What really pisses me off
Is she let me believe she was the one
And to think I thought that
Now how can I ever know?
It's the not knowing
That's the worst
'Jackson, do you like The Beatles?' Dita asks.
'Yeah, they went alright.'
'Me too. Do you know how John fell for Yoko?'
'Nope.'
'So, Yoko had an art exhibition in London. One of her pieces was a ladder, and at the base of the ladder was an invitation to climb it. And John Lennon rocked up to her exhibit. And he climbed the ladder. And when he got to the top, he found a magnifying glass hanging from the ceiling. And he took it and used it to look at a very small word that was taped to the ceiling. That word read, in tiny letters, *yes*. Not *no*. Not *fuck you*. Yes. Then, Lennon knew.'

The ride rocks up to Dita's apartment. She makes an immediate grab to open her door but stops before she does. She turns back to me.

'You're stuck in a deep hole, Jackson. And the sides are made of wet mud, and they're too slippery to climb. And the light hurts your eyes when you look up because you haven't had to look up for so long. But there's a ladder somewhere in the dark, I promise you. It's up to you and you alone to find it. Your friends have too much on their hands with just themselves.'

'You're lucky, you know? There's still a chance you'll never have to feel it.'

'Find the ladder, Jackson. Remember, Lennon died in love. Elvis died in vomit.'

****

I've been told by the driver that there are a fuck load of police blockades out tonight. He claims he knows this shortcut that he reckons will get me back to Max's joint quicker. I tell him that I'm not too fussed which way we end up going. I tell him that it doesn't make too much of a difference, not in the grand scheme of things.

The suburbs fall apart fast the further you move away from the city. We're weaving down some shitty industrial backblocks filled with factories and car yards and tile outlet stores, and we get stuck at a train level crossing. As the boom gates fall, the windows of the ride fog up. So much so, that I can't see anything outside. I use the sleeve of my coat to wipe the window clear just in time to see the train hurtle towards us. It flies past, carriage after carriage, until the night becomes still again, and the boom gates gently lift, as if there'd never been a train there at all.

> He surely would have known
> That it could have been you
> Who would find him there
> Still

I stare out the window as the industrial turns into suburbia, and houses and small shopfronts fly past. Then, in big red lights, I see THE SIN BIN written on the roof of some shithouse suburban bar. One of those ones with a car park out the front, filled with rubbish and recycling bins. I think of Max's house with the shitty front door with the broken lock or latch, and my freezing room with my air mattress that's developed a leak in the past week. And I think of waking up tomorrow morning and having to tiptoe between Max's puddles of piss on the cold bathroom floor just to brush my teeth. I lean forward to the driver.

'Can you pull over and let me out here. Cheers, mate.'

Chapter 33

I'm sitting at the bar with my beer. It's going down fast due to the lack of conversation interrupting my sips. The Sin Bin—what a fucken squalor. There are two old loose cuts, playing darts, whose stories clearly ended a couple of decades ago, and now the highlight of their week is shelving urinal cakes up their arses when they're lucky enough to find themselves in the men's room alone. A large family is wrapping up dinner festivities over in the corner. Kissing and hugging each other and all that shit. Some fucked up generational thing with everything from a baby still covered in afterbirth to an old lady slumped in a wheelchair, as close to death as one can be while still living. I can't work out which kid running around screaming is whose, what the occasion is, or why the hell they gave this miserable joint hosting honours.

'So,' I ask the bartender, 'this place pick up later?'

He's a mammoth of a man, pushing seven foot, sporting a broom moustache surrounded by five-day growth. His black hair is slicked back, and his hairy arms are drying schooner glasses on his red apron.

'Sometimes it does. Sometimes it doesn't,' he says in a deep, gruff voice. He places a dried glass back in the tray and reaches for a wet one. A woman, attractive, maybe mid-thirties, a brunette with a nice figure and slim jeans, walks up to the bar.

'What is it, Deb?' he asks her.

'House white, Baz.'

She smiles at me while the bartender bends down to fetch an open bottle from the fridge. He starts filling her glass, and I'm considering asking her how her night's going, but as soon as the bottle is pulled away from the rim she devours the drink in one scull. She slams a ten dollar note next to the empty glass and heads for the front door. For the first time, I see a young girl at her side, about the age of five, holding her mum's hand, trying hard to keep up with the manic walking pace of her mother as they exit the bar and disappear into the night.

'Good evening.'

A slender, ghostly figure has sat down in the stool next to me while my eyes were following Wine Glut out the door. There's so little to him that I didn't even hear him approach. He has a pale, unkempt look, as if he's crawled out from behind the rubbish and recycling bins out the front. He could pass as being in his final years of high school if it wasn't for his greying crew cut and the dark bags under his eyes that make the blue stand out more than they would otherwise. He's decked out in a green baggy jumper and black chinos, and he's wearing a pair of black leather driving gloves.

'How's it going,' I reply with muted enthusiasm.

'Haven't seen your face in here before,' he says.

'I'm staying with a mate around the corner, for a little bit.'

'I see. Well, that would explain why I have not seen you here before.'

He takes a sip of his whiskey, that I didn't even notice the bartender pour, and looks around the bar, as if he's looking for someone. But there's something off about him. Something not quite right. As if he's looking for someone who might be looking for him.

'Ah, life,' he says sad, but he picks himself up. 'Cheers!' and he bangs his whiskey glass into my bottle. 'And your name is?'

'Jackson.'

'Nice to meet you, Jackson. So, what do you do, Jackson?'

'Life Insurance.'

'I should see you about that sometime. Can be hazardous to one's health, life can.'

He tilts his head back and looks at me through squinted eyes.

'You know, Jackson. You look a little familiar. Did you go to Coburg High?'

'Nah. Albert Park Grammar.'

'Of course, you did, Jackson,' he winks. 'Of course, you did. Ah, life,' and his leg starts shaking.

'What's yours, then?' I ask.

'What's my what?'

'What's your name?'

'Why? What do you need to know my name for? You think you'll lose me in a place like this?' he says, looking over each shoulder. He leans into me and says under his breath, 'Trust me, Jackson, you won't.'

'Fucken hell, fine,' I sigh. 'I don't really care. I was just being polite.'

'Now you're feeling uncomfortable, aren't you? I can tell.'

'No.'

'Yes, you are. And you should. I know your name and your profession and what school you went to. And you? Well, whereas you, you don't even know my name.'

'I'll live.'

'Oh, will you just?'

I turn and look him in the eye. He breaks contact immediately and waves a finger in the air.

'Barry! Barry!' he yells. 'What's my name?'

Barry the Bartender is cutting lemons and limes with a large hunting knife and replies without looking up.

'Don't know. Don't care. Couldn't give a flying fuck, to tell you the truth.'

'And I've been coming here for years, Jackson. Always pay in cash too. Untraceable it is. As long as you don't stick your dirty prints all over it. Best investment I've ever made, these gloves. But no, Jackson. I'm not going to tell you my name. As you just heard then, I haven't even extended that courtesy to my best mate Barry there.'

'Fine,' I say.

'You want another beer?' he asks. 'Let me shout you a beer.'

'Nah, it's okay. I don't like owing anything to others.'

'I said it's my shout. Yes, it's true, the term has been bastardised somewhat in recent years. But I can assure you, I do mean that it would be my shout, in its purest essence: No need to buy me back. Barry! Another beer for Jackson here, and one for myself too.'

'Honestly, it's okay,' I say, but the hunting knife has already popped the lids of two bottles that have been slammed down in front of us.

'Of course,' he goes on, 'most people will use someone's name to assert authority in a conversation, like I did to Barry then when I ordered my beer.'

'Fucken nutcase,' Barry's had enough and walks off to serve a loose cut.

'But, Jackson. I will, at the very least, tell you what I do.'

Our conversation falls silent for a minute or so.

'So?' I say. 'Are you going to tell me?'

'Tell you what?'

'What you do?'

'Ah, there you go. The anticipation!' He puts his hand on my shoulder and shakes me. 'Savour this moment, Jackson. Breathe it in through your nose and out through your mouth.'

'You know what? I think I might go sit over there for a bit. Cheers for the beer.'

'Oh yeah? And what are you gonna do over there? Hang out with your other mates? Where are they right now?'

'Look, mate. I just came here for a quiet drink.'

'Don't even try to get that shit past me, Jackson. That's the last fucken thing you came here for. I'm not some cunt you can bullshit. That's the last thing I am.'

I step off my bar stall, and he grabs my arm.

'You'll wanna let the fuck go, mate,' I say. 'I'm not even fucken kidding.'

And he does.

'Okay, okay. Touchy one, aren't you, Jackson? Okay, I'll tell you what I do. Sit, please. Sit, sit. Drink your beer. Drink, drink.'

'I'm not going to buy you one back.'

'It's okay. I always mean what I say. It was my shout. It's all good.'

'It fucken better be.'

'Okay, Jackson. The truth is this: I deal in the truth.'

'Fucken hell. If this is some more existential garbage, this is not the night. All this reiki bullshit has fucked up enough lives already.'

'No, no, no. None of that. See, I view truths as commodities. They exist. There's a want for them, and in some particularly morbid cases: a need. And consumers, in return, are willing to pay for them.'

'Fuck me.'

'Okay, I can see you're sensitive about this matter. Let me do a better job of explaining it.'

'You'll wanna hurry the fuck up about it.'

'I'm getting there, Jackson. Please, stay with me. Okay, we all present an edited version of ourselves to the world, to our friends, our family, our workmates. To our other. We play the role we want others to believe.'

'What are you into? Blackmailing cunts?'

'No, no, no. Absolutely not. The opposite, really.'

'Because not everyone's got something to hide, you know?'

'But everyone's got a truth they want to know.'

'So, what does this have to do with what you do?'

'I find that truth. That's my job.'

'You're a private eye?'

'Of sorts.'

'You follow people around all day?'

'No. God, no. I've got too much on my hands to do that.'

'So, what's your source, then?'

'People. Inside contacts, mostly. You'd be surprised how stagnant the wages are of people protecting your personal data. Makes them susceptible to certain external influences,' and he rubs the finger and thumb of his black driving glove together in my face.

'This some sort of sales spiel, is it?'

'Any truth. Found. Guaranteed. So, tell me, Jackson. What keeps you up at night?'

I'm trying to read this guy. I'm waiting for a catch, a punch line, a 'just kidding, mate.' And I tap my pockets to feel my wallet and phone to make sure he hasn't lifted them. But as this place is dead, and he's mildly intriguing, I play with him some more.

'So, tell me how it all works.'

'No money upfront. Payment on delivery of the truth. Cash in a brown paper bag. I'm somewhat of a Luddite, you see. No refunds, though, if the truth is not to your liking. It's rarely the case, to be honest. But still, peace of mind, right? Hard to put a price on that. So, what truth does your mind want, Jackson? Or maybe you're one of those sick ones who needs it.'

I take a steep sip of my beer.

'Ah, yes!' he says all excited. 'What was her name?'

'How much?'

'Five thousand dollars.'

'Fucken hell, five grand?'

'Hey, hey, hey. I need to pay people who pay people, remember. Five grand and you'll know everything. I like to keep my rates accessible to Joe Public. Trust me, one day you'll look back on all this and consider it the bargain of a lifetime. All I need is a name.'

> Through sickness she promised
> And still
> She told him
> He had to leave

'All I need is a name, Jackson.'

A moment.

'Chelsea.'

He stands up and holds out his hand.

I shake it.

'So, what now?' I ask. 'Do we swap numbers?'

'No. I don't have a phone. They're a liability. That's another truth on the house for you. Now that you're a highly esteemed client of mine, you're entitled to these free industry insights. However, Jackson, my new friend, I must apologise to you. I just remembered I've got to be somewhere that's not here. And so, I shall bid you a fond farewell. Lovely to meet you, Jackson.'

'But how do we stay in touch?'

'Name, profession, school. That's at least two more than I need, trust me.'

'You know what? Maybe let me sleep—'

'I'll stop you there, Jackson. This whole little arrangement does come with a little disclaimer,' and he leans in and whispers in my ear. 'Best honour the handshake. I can be your blessing or your curse. You choose.'

He tucks in his bar stool and points at the bar, 'Great to see you, Barry. You make this establishment what it is.'

Then he turns back to me, shaking his finger like he's forgotten something.

'One more thing, Jackson. What would you like to name me?'

'What would I like to name you?'

'What would you like my name to be?'

'Why?'

'So, I can say who's calling when I call.'

'I'll call you Blank.'

'Blank? I like that. That's a clever one. You're a sharp tool, Jackson.'

And he's out the front door and into the night.

****

I wake up just after four-in-the-morning with the light still on in my room. I'm fully clothed, lying on top of my sleeping bag, and I'm fucken freezing. Barry the Bartender wasn't lying. Sometimes the place does go off. A little after eleven, it started to pack out. I was deep into beers by then and only just holding my conversation together. I started talking to a group of girls who rocked up to the bar on a hen's night. I explained to them that I was with a friend earlier, but he fell ill and left, which is why I was there alone. I could sense Barry's disapproval at my mistruth as he poured the Chartreuse shots I bought the whole fucken lot of them. I hung out with them a while, even got drunk enough to dance, and ended up making out with one of them, but she told me she had to go to the bathroom to find one of her friends and promised me she would come straight back but never did. And when I got tired of dancing by myself, I went back to Barry and drank some more beer, faster. It really was going down like water because I had nowhere else to be and nothing to do Sunday. Plenty of time to nurse a hangover, so no logical reason to slow down. It would all help to prolong my sleep in anyway. And when the ugly lights came on at one-in-the-morning, and Barry told everyone to get out and fuck off, I staggered down the street and knocked on the door of the 7-Eleven. An older man with a long grey beard came out in his pyjamas and dressing gown, and he unlocked the door for me, and I tried to use the tongs to put a donut in the paper bag, but the tongs were way too slippery for my liking, and the donut fell on the ground, and the dressing gown guy, somewhat disgusted at my state, asked me to point out which flavour I wanted (pink), and he did it all for me and sent me on my way. I can't even remember if I paid, to be honest. I think he was just pleased to see the back of me.

I've woken up, I realise, because Max must have burst loudly through the front door. Inconsiderate fuck. I can hear him bouncing off the hallway walls, literally telling himself off.

'Look how much money you spent tonight, Max. You dumb fuck! Pissed it all up a fucken wall again. Fuck Trent, fuck him. The cunt.'

And very quietly, light footed so I don't draw attention to my awake state, I switch off the light and climb into my sleeping bag. My head's spinning backwards at an ill angle, drilling down into my pillow, and I pray that the hangover taxman will pass over me tomorrow. Maybe some clerical error on his behalf, an office oversight, and I'll awake surprisingly refreshed, all things considering. But the early onset of beer sweats hints otherwise, and I'm forced to flip my pillow onto its cold side to give my flush face some temporary relief from the heat rising within.

Chapter 34

Lorne, Part One

Those lips that Love's own hand did make,
Breathed forth the sound that said 'I hate',
To me that languished for her sake:
But when she saw my woeful state,
Straight in her heart did mercy come,
Chiding that tongue that ever sweet,
*Was use**d in** giving gentle doom;*
And taught it thus anew to greet;
'I hate' she altered with an end,
That followed it as gentle day,
Doth follow night, who like a fiend
From heaven to hell is flown away.
'I hate', from hate away she threw,
And saved my life, saying 'not you.'
William Shakespeare, d. 1616.

Saturday Morning. The rain lashes hard at the window. I slip out of my sleeping bag and step onto the freezing borer-ravaged floorboards. The city has imposed itself so heavily on my psych in recent weeks that I'm beyond ready to escape its grasp. I walk down the hallway and bang hard on Max's door.

'Oi! Wake the fuck up, cunt!'

I want to get on the road before eight in the hope that we don't hit any traffic. It's also so that I don't have to see all those depressing new suburbs built next to the highway in full light. This is a confirmed two-up mission. Neither of us has heard from Trent during the week, and Bones has dropped right off the radar altogether. We figured it best to leave him in peace until he sorts himself out. Max opens his bedroom door, only as wide as half his face.

'What time is it?' he yawns.

'Fucken hell, Max. I told you last night I wanted to get on the road before eight. Did you set your alarm like I told you to?'

'Calm down. Give me five, then.'

****

We're on the road, finally, after Max fucked around packing longer than he needed to. The wipers are working hard as he drives us out of suburbia, around the outskirts of the city, and we link up with the M1, and I can feel all the shit of the city break off me as the skyline gets smaller in the rear view. Sometimes you just need to throw some money at a situation, and this is one of those times. It's only a one-night mission, so I've sorted somewhere nice to stay. A nice four-star hotel on the beach at Lorne. It's winter, so they put up their rooms for fuck all. My shout, for Max letting me stay as long as I have without him asking me once for rent or to pitch in for toilet paper or anything like that. Mostly, I'm just thirsty to experience what nice is like again. A clean shower and bath. A shitless toilet. Soft sheets, pillows with pillow cases, artwork on the walls. To feel again, for a moment, something of what I had. To check in on that way of things so I don't stray too far from it that I'll never be able to find it again.

Bon Scott is screaming at us through the tin can speakers of Max's white Seat Ibiza, built well before airbags. Only a faded dashboard offers protection from the flying asphalt beneath us while, out the window, cheese-cutter barriers chainsaw at our sides. The car shakes violently when it gets close to a hundred, so we have to cruise ten below that. We're in the outside lane, but we're constantly being overtaken by angry cunts on the inside, honking the horn and flying the finger. It's blowing a gale too, so Max has to turn the steering wheel hard into the wind to keep the car in the lane. There's a dark cloud brooding over the mountains of the You Yangs. One of those monster waves of rain that I know will crash down on us soon. The birds know it too. Large flocks of them are flying all over the place like fucken maniacs. A road train, a big massive fucker, flies past us doing at least fifty over the limit. Water sprays from its tires so intensely that Max can't see where he's going. Way too much water for the thin little wipers to cope with. Slowly the windscreen drains, and as soon as we see the road again, some big fucken hawk swoops at us, and Max has to swerve into the next lane to miss it.

'Fucken hell,' I say. 'What was his end game?'

'Sniffing for roadkill,' Max says.

'His nose would have known about it if he got any closer.'

'So, I'll tell ya an interesting story,' Max says. 'There's this caretaker at work. He owns this bible on chasing ladies, and he's been trying all year to get the perfect seven. You know what the perfect seven is?'

'No,' I sigh.

'Seven girls, seven nights, one week.'

'How's that going for him?'

'He reckons he's had six in a row, ten times. But the seventh one always falls over at the final hurdle.'

We drive another couple of kilometres in silence.

'So, how does the story end, then?'

'Nah, that's it. That's the story. He never got to seven.'

'Jesus Christ, Max. What kind of story was that? What do you want? My sympathy?'

'It's just an interesting story, I thought. Some sort of modern-day Dionysian tragedy.'

'Well, it's a work of fucken fiction, I'll give you that.'

'Yeah, well, each to their own I guess. He lent it to me once, that dating book.'

'Yeah? How'd that go for you? Your hot girlfriend waiting for us in Lorne, is she?'

'Must have read it the wrong way up or something.'

'Anyway, I've never got these blokes who obsess over numbers. Unless you're getting all Attenborough about labia, it's all one and the same, as far as I'm concerned.'

'Maybe some guys just want to get as far away from single as possible,' Max says.

****

We pull up at the service station to fill up the tank, which I specifically asked Max to do last night, but, of course, he forgot. Max, with his small frame, needs two hands to wrestle the petrol nozzle free from its holster. He grits his teeth and grunts as he rams the nozzle into the petrol hole at the back of the Ibiza.

With Trent and Bones failing to get a start on this trip, it's a given that a majority of the conversation for the next two hours will inevitably involve various forms of dissection of the absentees, if not straight out assassination. It's the same when you leave the table to take a piss with any of this lot. The best you can pray for is that a slim shred of your being is still left intact by the time you return.

'Given the choice, who would you put first before the Bali firing squad?' Max asks. 'Trent or Bones?'

'Trent would be first,' I say. 'Then Bones. That would be my clear order. That's assuming first is worst. If I could be certain that Trent would get upset at seeing Bones's brain matter splattered across the shooting yard tarp, fully comprehensive of the inevitability of his own impending execution, well, in that case, I'd happily reverse the order.'

'Fair reasoning,' Max says.

We're back on the road. I'm sipping my servo sewer coffee, and Max has his cup between his legs because his car was built well before cup holders too. The coffee tastes even worse than it usually does. It somehow loses even more flavour against the tired interior. Nigel Lassiter is on the radio—again—this time flogging shampoo.

'From the tropical forests of Papua New Guinea, comes Cocoda Shampoo. Made from coffee beans and the world's purest organic coconut oil. Sourced from coconuts handpicked by native tribesmen, who climb the tree of life with their bare hands. Available now at all leading supermarkets.'

'So, what do you make of Trent's state-of-affairs?' I ask.

'Now, Trent's problems are many,' Max says. 'When he goes out, he's still using the same techniques that he used when he was sixteen and pashing up birds at parties down the side of the house, by the rubbish and recycling bins. High fives, shots, drinking games. Crazy, wacky dancing. He can't get an emotional connection with a girl because he's so focussed on all these superficial shortcuts. Don't get me wrong, I admire his resolve in the face of rejection. But if I've seen him do the cold approach at bars, you know, that do or die table invasion, if I've seen him do it a hundred times, I've seen it come off once, maybe twice. If that. And by come off, I mean he wasn't told to fuck off. I look away now when he does it. Creates too much doubt in my own mind, seeing him fail over and over again. Bad for the psych, I reckon. Now when he does it, I just stare down the neck of my beer and wait for him to slink back onto his stool.'

We run into a traffic jam. It's a bad one. We're stuck on the outskirts of the city, crawling slow enough that I begin to notice the subtle differences between the uniformed orange rooves peeking up from behind the vandalised concrete walls. A slightly different shade of orange, a slightly different shape of aerial, the only way to tell one poor cunt's pad from his neighbours. I don't blame the folks who live in these places. Far from it. They're doing the best they can under some tough fucken circumstances. It's those greedy Xer land-developer cunts that I've got my eye on. Even worse than those boomers in many ways. Short memories the Xers, that's for fair fucken certain. Too busy researching jet skis and family holidays in Bora Bora to give one flying fuck about how their junk houses look to the living and passing. At least Max's grotty old place has character. Takes more than one sentence to describe his shithole. I'll tip the hat to it for that.

'As for Bones,' Max goes on. 'Breakups make bodybuilders. I don't think he ever recovered after that American one never returned. I don't think he saw that one coming. But the fact of the matter is this, Jackson: Both Japan and USA were here on a fucken holiday. That's not real life. It's not. Every time I hear some wanderlusting, fernwahing cunt run their tongue, I think: You scared, piss weak, sack-of-shit. It's all a ruse of their own creation. You can only run from this life shit for so long until it tracks down your address and kicks in your front door. And granted, it seems Bones's Japan one is still kicking about town. But here forever? Fucken doubt it. One bout of homesickness and she's one-waying her way back to her home province with a thirty-kilo suitcase in each hand.'

Max turns down the radio and continues, 'Regardless of any minor discrepancies, my point is this: We've been born on some desert island a million fucken miles away from anywhere. That's all we are to most others. A fantasy for a couple of years until they all fly back home to get on with things. It's easy to forget that sometimes.'

We crawl past the accident that's caused the traffic jam, and our ravaging of Bones's life choices is spared for the moment as we fall silent and try to get our heads around exactly what happened. A police officer in a bright yellow raincoat ushers the cars around road cones with a wave of his hand as four lanes painfully merge into one. Another officer is in deep conversation with an ambulance driver. Some rubberneckers in front of us stick their heads out of their windows to take in the full horror of the scene, and I tell Max to wind down his foggy window too so we can get a decent look at what they're all looking at. A crumpled shell of a burnt-out hatchback lies under the teeth of a monstrous road train, swallowed and spat out, blackened and smouldering, even in the constant torrential rain. Four firefighters spray their foam guns over the mess.

'Well, they're dead,' Max says.

'You'd fucken well hope so,' I say.

And I contemplate her reaction had it been us, ten minutes earlier and two lanes over.

I hope I would haunt her.

I really hope I would.

The scene falls beyond the rotational capacity of our necks, and the traffic in front of us picks up speed again. Max puts his foot down hard on the pedal, the engine screaming as he tries his best to bring the Ibiza back up towards a civil ninety.

'Fucken hell, I think the fucken clutch is going,' he says.

'Whose lot would you have, then?' I ask. 'Trent or Bones?'

'Bones. Without a doubt.'

'What? Even with all this Belarus business?'

'At least Bones has a story. Trent's story is he has no story. He'd never admit it, but I know it keeps him up at night. I know for sure, it does. I mean, that's more than half the cunt's problem. What the fuck do you talk about when you have no story? Chartreuse, Jackson. Chartreuse is what you talk about.'

Cloned houses turn into factories and abattoirs and pylons, and those, in time, turn into eucalyptus trees and lush fields made green by winter. And we escape free, through the roundabout at Torquay and under the wooden archway of the Great Ocean Road, snaking our way along the coastline, rising and falling above the bays and beaches as traffic piles up behind us every time a passing lane ends. Angry faces in our mirror, pissed off at being forced to wait all of five fucken minutes until the next chance to fly the finger.

'Ah, fuck!' Max says, slamming his fist hard on the steering wheel. 'Fuck! Forgot to put out the fucken rubbish bin again. Fuck!'

Chapter 35

Lorne, Part Two

'Everyone shut the fuck up and piss off,' the bouncer screams.

We're standing outside Lorne Tavern. It's a few minutes past one-in-the-morning, and the bouncer keeps yelling at us to fuck off because everyone's speaking at the top of their voices and it'll give fodder to the boomer cunts who own holiday homes here and want Lorne Tavern shutdown because of all the noise.

'Well?' Sophia says in her English accent. 'Are you coming with us, then?'

She puts her black beanie on, taming flames of red hair that lick down her front. It's the last ride back to Erskine Falls Backpackers. Of course, Max and I aren't checked-in there, but the poor cunt who's somehow copped a career in driving the backpacker courtesy van doesn't know this. He's running around trying to round up the scattered and drunk and get them into the back of his van. I'd call him mid-thirties. A beanpole frame growing out of a pair of skate shoes that haven't been white in a while. Denim shorts that hang over his knees, a red crew-neck T, a black NY flat cap, and that's it. In the middle of fucken winter. You know, out of the thousand or so skateboarding fuckwits I've seen attempting kickflips and ollies on the steps of the State Library, I can't recall one cunt landing one trick once. Anyway, in this dark hour, it would be near impossible for Skatey Driver to tell us apart from the usual eclectic mess of international travellers who grace this beachside town for one night with their gross intoxication, other than our local accents that I'm conscious of keeping out of earshot. Sophia's two friends have already taken their seats in the back of the van, but Sophia's still standing by the van door.

'Decision time, Jackson. Yes or no.'

****

Earlier today, when we checked into our swish hotel on the beach, there was some confusion from the old duck behind the desk. Turned out some cunt, without my knowing, had upgraded us to some fucken honeymoon suite, when I specifically booked the two-bedroom economy room.

'Look, there's no fucken way I'm sharing a queen bed with that cunt,' I told her.

'Oh, I'm terribly sorry,' Old Duck replied. 'I picked you two as a couple of those fairy folk,' and she started cackling to herself like some fucken hayseed.

I hit back at her.

'No fucken skin off my nose you thought we were a couple. It's just I shared a tent with this cunt one New Year's Eve, and he shat his sleeping bag, and I promised myself never again.'

Jesus Christ, you get all sorts of yokel types out this way. Anyway, Old Duck clicked a few things on her computer and sorted it all out in the end. We checked into our two-bedroom economy room, and for a moment, just for a passing moment, I felt a sense of home. Clean carpet, firmly-made beds, bedside lamps, a spotless bathroom with nice towels and hand cloths even, a bathmat that's the same colour as the towels, all those little bottles of shampoo and conditioner and bodywash in a cute little basket on the vanity. And in the top drawer beside the bed, a bible. I didn't pick it up, but it was nice to know it was there. The room had a good view of the sea too. We went outside onto the little balcony and watched the Southern Ocean roll in all angry, sea spray exploding over the shoreline, and we sat there and watched it all for a while, the waves roll in, set after set, as the rain set in. We just sat there, without saying a word, until we tired of each other's company and decided to hit up Lorne Tavern.

It was pissing down by the time we got there. Meant it was so busy inside that we were forced to share one of those long wooden tables with others. Good, in that girls were sitting down, but bad in that other blokes were too. Two large blokes sat down right next to us. Not lanky. Not fat. The same proportions as normal blokes but stretched out in every direction. I picked them straight away as country boys moving to the city to make big. I could fucken smell it on them. One of them was a loud, mouthy cunt, going on and on about how they can only call it Champagne if it comes from France. Him and his mate were flinging around some flutes because a horse they have a micro-share in, ran a place in some country meet on some dust track I've never fucken heard of.

'This Mo-ay here,' he said. 'This is the real stuff.'

I let the first one fly, but he kept at me.

'Look!' he said, holding up the bottle of Moët for the table. 'Says it on the tin. Mo-ay and Shan-don, Sham-pain.'

'Et,' I said. 'Fucken, et.'

'What?'

'Moët: rhymes with poet.'

Why he didn't just leave it there, I don't know.

'They don't sound the T in French, mate,' he told me.

'You want your fucken ducks in a row when you come at me, cunt,' I said. 'The name Moët is Dutch. The Dutch don't elide the T, you fucken pagan.'

I possibly over did it, how I said it, because the big fulla didn't say much again for the rest of the night. Went all weird and quiet. Just sat there sipping his flute in silence. I felt a bit bad for a bit, right after I said it, but my spray got me the attention of this English girl called Sophia. She introduced herself from across the table in an accent that seemed slower than necessary but kind on the ear.

'You speak other languages?' she asked me.

'Yes.'

'Me too.'

Turned out she's taken more than a half glance at a whiteboard too. We continued our conversation across the table, and when Max went to the men's room, she snaked his seat next to me. Sophia's story is that she's been in Australia closing in on eleven months. She came over after she wrapped up things at Cambridge. Flew into Sydney, worked six months as a waitress at Bondi Beach, and then she backpacked her away around the perimeter of Australia. Byron Bay; Fraser Island; Whitsundays; Great Barrier Reef; the Daintree Forest; across to Darwin; down to Broome; then Perth; Adelaide for an afternoon; and now it's her last night on the road before she hits Melbourne for a week. Then it's back home to London for good. She could stay here another year, but that would require her to do the mandatory three months of farm work to extend her working holiday visa which we both agreed would not be her thing. I think it's insulting that we make them do that. I told Sophia that if it was the other way around, and her lot tried to make me go up to the tip of Scotland to pick thistle all day, I'd tell the whole kingdom to go fuck themselves.

Sophia's travelling with two friends. If Trent was here, he'd call them Silver and Bronze. Neither of them seemed to take too much of an interest in Max, though. He tried his best to spark up some conversation, and even when it died on him, as it often did, to Max's credit, he kept on bashing the flint. He really did try his best tonight. And then I noticed another other. In the corner of the bar, sitting alone, no drink in front of him. His eyes staring death at me. Sophia noticed me noticing him and told me not to worry about him. But I've seen those eyes before. Goon Zombie.

****

'Get in the bloody van, Jackson,' Sophia orders.

The bouncer throws the last patron out of Lorne Tavern by his collar and belt, 'Home time, ya cunt!'

'Max, you coming?' I ask.

'Dunno, man,' Max says. 'Still getting over the flu. I was kinda looking forward to getting a decent night's sleep, to be honest.'

'You'll get plenty of sleep at Coburg cemetery one day. Get in the fucken van.'

I'm not sure why Max is being so hesitant at present. He used to throw himself teeth-first into situations like these, back in the day. And I wouldn't say it's totally dead in the water for him with the other two, so he still has some hope in hell of finding company tonight. Max and I take a couple of spare seats in the middle of the van, and we squash up tight as the last of the legitimate paid guests of the backpackers pour in behind us, until all seats are taken. Skatey Driver is looking all confused as he leans in through the van door.

'Ah, excuse me,' he says, staring at his clipboard. 'Is everyone here staying at Erskine Falls Backpackers?'

'Yes!' the collective yells back at him with utter contempt for the cunt's question.

He's got an Australian accent, Skatey Driver does. Jesus Christ. When you're working at a backpackers in your own fucken country, you can be sure as hell your life hasn't gone to plan. Max and I have clearly thrown out his numbers, so Goon Zombie, who up until this point has been loitering in the shadows by the rubbish and recycling bins, is forced to sit upfront next to Skatey Driver. Fuck knows which country shat out Goon Zombie. He's an ill looking bloke with a similar build to me, but he's not copped a pair of clippers in a fair few months. Not the type of hair that looks good long, either. Brown mangy hair that's grown out rather than down. Probably some personal protest against the office job that did his head in before he started travelling the world. The death eyes he's been making at me all night have yet to cease, and as the courtesy van splutters up the steep road towards the dark hills, Goon Zombie turns around and throws me another set for good luck.

****

Goon Zombies, you'll find them everywhere. Often English, not always though, who arrive in Australia, and no word of a lie, I know of Englishmen and Englishwomen who have broken down crying in aisles the first time they saw the price of piss in Australia. Grown pomegranates bawling their eyes out. Because in their planning of their extensive and detailed budget required to circumnavigate this massive fucken island, they had failed to account for the considerable tax the Governor-General has placed on our beer, wine, and spirits. And for the ladies and gentlemen who come from afar to visit our land of golden soil, bondage, and tyranny, and who inevitably find themselves in less than favourable financial circumstances, the answer always has been, and always will be: Goon—wine in a box. A box that warns you in small print that its contents may contain traces of crustaceans. Truth. Now, you can do one night on the goon and wear the worst hangover of your life. But weeks, even months on it, as some poor cunts are forced to do, that will change the person you are. It will literally kill your soul. And so, all those who do, sooner or later, become Goon Zombies. They're the ones you really gotta worry about. The ones that have checked out already but are still here.

****

Erskine Falls Backpackers lies deep within the rainforest of Otway National Park. Everyone falls all over each other as Skatey Driver takes the courtesy van through every corner at a furious speed, tracing the road through the rolling hills. I've found my fucken seatbelt, but I can't find it's fucken latch, and I'm digging under Max's arse, but I'm still not having any fucken luck finding this fucken latch, and I just hope this fucken joke running the show upfront knows how to keep this fucken van on the fucken road. I don't know where we're going to sleep tonight, but Sophia must be a mind reader or something because she taps my shoulder from the seat behind and tells me not to worry. Whispers to me that it'll all work itself out. I'm not as drunk as I normally would be by now, as my conversation with Sophia slowed down my drinking, as this talk thing tends to do. That's why I'm still thinking about things like seatbelts and where I'm going to sleep tonight.

'Why didn't we just invite them back to the hotel room?' Max whispers to me under his breath.

'Because, Max,' I say, 'that would have been fucken creepy. Way too on the nose. You need to get your head around these things fucken quick. Might give you a shot at getting a girlfriend one day.'

We turn off the main road and the wheels crunch up a steep gravel driveway. Skatey Driver slams the courtesy van into a low whiny gear, and we bump our way up and around even tighter corners for the next ten minutes, until we arrive at a clearing in front of Erskine Falls Backpackers. It's a whole lot of connected cabins built into the side of a steep hill, nestled between dingo dens and under a canopy of eucalyptus trees filled with drop bears. He slides open the van door and we pile out. It's snowing.

'Bet ya never thought it snowed in Ozzie, mate,' Skatey Driver says to me.

I chuck him a smile and a thumbs up. Sophia's smiling and catching the flakes in her mittens, and I'm starting to doubt she's thought things through much more beyond this. Goon Zombie is hanging around on the edge of our group, but he's stopped making eyes at me. Now both of them are set on Sophia. He walks up to her, totally ignoring me. He gets really close to her and leans into her ear and asks her in broken English if he can talk to her alone. She tells him between gritted teeth that they don't need to talk because there's nothing to talk about. He tugs her arm. She pulls it away and tells him that she's said all she needed to say. Maybe it's a crush, maybe they hooked up last night. At this point, it doesn't concern me. All I know is this: I have her attention and he doesn't. And I enjoy this feeling. I would love to tell the cunt to fuck off right here, right at this very moment, but technically I'm not a guest here, so I send my teeth through my tongue and uphold an illusion of calmness. I'm certain my appearance of poise will add to his torment anyway, so I'll take it as a win of sorts. Goon Zombie walks away, chin on chest, and I see him look over his shoulder a couple of times before he creeps off into the dark to find his bunk amongst the warren of cabins burrowed into the bush.

'Right, we need some beverages,' Sophia says. 'This way, gentlemen.'

We follow her and her two friends up the steps, past the reception desk, and into the communal kitchen blanketed in stainless steel. Inside one of the grotty old fridges, between yesterday's tomato pasta and tomorrow's toast, are a whole lot of goon boxes. Sophia passes one to each of us.

'I can't vouch for their vintage,' she says.

'These all yours?' I ask.

'I'll buy them back tomorrow. There, that should do us.'

'You'd fucken hope so.'

'Remember, we have to be quiet, though.'

The three girls are in a female-only, four-bed dorm with two bunkbeds. The fourth occupant is a German girl called Eva, who I'm told has to get up early for a long waterfall hike. The girls turn on the light. Eva stirs in her top bunk under a white blanket. Sophia, thankfully, has secured the bottom bunk, so I kick off my shoes and sit down on hers. Max takes a seat under the window between the bunks, next to an old radiator heater that offers warmth. Eva, to her credit, is incredibly tolerable of our invasion at this late hour, and we return the courtesy by turning off the lights and continuing our conversation and goon drinking in attempted whispers, and when I run out of words, I kiss Sophia.

Chapter 36

Lorne, Part Three

It's deep into the night, and Sophia and I are still drinking from our goon boxes that are close to being half demolished. I'm so full that I feel I'm now just drinking to keep ahead of the hangover, possibly to outrun it even. Though, deep down, I'm aware of the probable failure of this logic. I think both of Sophia's friends have either coma'd or gone to sleep, and Eva is snoring, so she's happy enough with her lot. Right now, in this pitch-black dorm room, I'm just enjoying the peace of the moment. And I haven't thought of this until now, but I haven't heard from Max for at least a half hour. I can just make out his silhouette, slumped under the window.

'Max,' I whisper.

Unresponsive.

'Max!'

'Shh, inside voices,' Sophia says.

Unresponsive.

'Fuck's sake,' I say. 'Max!'

I get up from Sophia's bunk, and the bed-springs shriek loud enough that Eva stops snoring and thrashes a bit under her blanket.

'Fuck, sorry,' I say.

I walk across the room, and my sudden struggle with this two-leg balancing act registers for the first time how much I may have had to drink tonight. I trip over a hair straightener or something.

'Fuck, sorry,' I tell Sophia.

'Voices,' Sophia says.

I walk up to Max, lean down, and put my hand on his shoulder.

'Max, mate. You alive?'

It's dark, but I can see that his chin is slumped on his shoulder. I pick up the goon box at his side, and the whole fucken thing is empty.

'I think he's a bit coma'd,' I whisper back to Sophia.

'He'll be okay there,' she says.

'Max, mate. You okay there?'

Unresponsive.

I tiptoe back through the mess of bleeding backpacks and lie back down on Sophia's bunk, slowly so it doesn't creak, and as soon as my back hits the bedding, I hear a groan from the dark depths of Max's soul.

'Max,' I say. 'You okay, mate?'

And I hear soft spurts of vomit escaping his mouth. For a moment the room holds still.

Darkness.

Silence.

Peace.

Only for a moment. Then, concentrated by the confined space, the sickly odour of vomit consumes every molecule of fresh air in this female-only, four-bed dorm.

'Bloody hell,' Sophia yells. 'Get him out of here!'

I resist switching on the light, the only courtesy I can still give to the paid guests. In close to complete darkness, I scamper over to Max. My volume is the least of my concerns now. With one hand I grip the hood of his hoody, and with the other I grab the belt of his jeans. And I start dragging him out of the room, over the hair straighteners, catching him on all the charging phones, through the sprawled clothes and underwear, and it's only when I throw him out into the light of the corridor that I can get a true look at the state he's in. His limbs are limp, as if his bones want fuck all to do with things at this moment. His face is red and sweaty, and his eyes, when they open for a fleeting moment, are rolled back into his head. All down the front of his hoody is chunky, white vomit the consistency of overcooked porridge, some of which I've managed to get on my hands. I suspect Max's current state would soon be frowned upon by backpacker security, so I start dragging him by both arms down the long corridor towards the men's room. He's heavier than he looks, Max is, and I have to stop halfway to catch my breath. I ram my back into the men's room door and drag him across the piss-soaked floor and throw him into the far cubicle. I grab his sweaty hair and roughly position his head over the bowl.

'There,' I tell him. 'You fucken throw up in there, when you have to.'

Unresponsive.

I leave him to be in the cubicle and walk across to the basins to wash his sick off my hands. I look at the mirror. Some travelling poet has scratched a messy 'FUCK YOU' in the top left corner. Fucken shameless, some people are. My eyes and ears appear red, my skin seems thin, and I notice cavernous creases in my forehead that I've never noticed before. I hear Max heave, followed by a splatter in the bowl. I splash some water on my face, but I still look just as bad, only wetter now. I plant both hands on the sink bench, lean into the mirror, and look at myself even closer, right in my bloodshot eyes.

'Look at me will you, Chelsea?' I spit under my breath. 'Look where I've ended up, will you?'

And I hear the bathroom door open, and it's Sophia coming in to see if we're okay. Only it's not. Instead of her, it's him. He's standing there, smiling. Goon Zombie. An unsettling smiling, like his eyes aren't quite on the same page. He parks himself up at the urinal, and I continue washing my hands. I give them a shake and move over to the hand dryer. It's one of those old ones, and it makes a fierce old growling noise when it fires up. And I start to feel the back of my jeans getting wet. A warm wet. I turn around, and Goon Zombie is standing there with a big smile on his face and his dick hanging out, pissing on my feet.

'That's what you are, mate,' he says. 'A toilet. I piss on you.'

'Mother fucker,' I say, raising my fist.

'Whoa, whoa, mate,' he says, shaking his dick on me. 'Are you reserved here? Who the police believe, mate?'

And he slugs me in the guts. The air rushes out of my lungs. I stagger back, keeled over, and the tiled wall catches me. Goon Zombie slaps a hug on me, and I have no breath left to fight or to argue otherwise.

'It's okay. I'm not mad,' he says, pulling me closer, cradling my head to his chest and stroking my hair. 'It's only every time I need to talk to Sophia, you talk with her.'

And his knee plunges into my sack. I collapse to the ground, breaking my fall with my hand that slides across his puddle of piss. And I have no air in my lungs to cry out from the piercing dagger that's imbedded in my intestines. And I try to speak, my mouth gasping for air, my lungs screaming, pleading for a breath.

You walked into the bathroom

And saw your dad's eyes

Hanging by tendons

From the bloody mound that was his face

His gun on the tiled floor

You have your father's eyes

Your mother would say

Help

Help

Help

And my throat relaxes, and I take a big breath, and my lungs refill with oxygen. Glorious, glorious oxygen.

'Help! Max!'

There's a murmur from the cubicle, and I hear him pinballing off the walls, and Max staggers out with full momentum, as if he's been pushed out by his sober ghost. He runs at Goon Zombie and takes the two of them aerial, and they land hard against the men's room door. Max wrestles on top of him, his hands around Goon Zombies neck. I stagger to my feet and stumble over to them.

'Help,' Goon Zombie yells out to the corridor. 'Hel—'

And I smash him in the face as hard as I can, and he shuts up. Max releases his grip, and I drag Goon Zombie by his long scummy backpacker hair to the far cubicle. He's groggy and moaning, and I chuck his face right into Max's spew. When I let him come up for air, he gasps, 'Help,' and then he spews on Max's spew, and I plunge his whole fucken face back into the dual layers of sick, the smell of it all nearly making me throw up over him too.

'Enough, Jackson!' Max yells. 'Let him go. I can't get dragged into this shit. I teach children, for fuck's sake!'

'Fine,' I say, catching my breath. 'Fine.'

'We gotta get out of here,' Max says, all agitated. 'We've got to go now, mate. We've got to.'

'Alright, mate. Calm down. Jesus.'

And we're sprinting down the corridor to our escape, and I throw open the door to Sophia's dorm as we pass.

'Sophia!'

The others stir in their bunks from the light I've thrown into the room from the corridor. The whole room still reeks of Max's sick, so some of it has clearly caught something. Sophia sits up all confused.

'What is it?' she asks.

'What's your last name?'

'Why? What's going on?'

'I've got to go,' I say. 'Your last name. What is it?'

'Why? What's happened?'

She gets up and turns on the light. Eva groans. Max is up ahead, dancing on the spot, all worried about getting caught.

'Fucken hurry the fuck up, Jackson!' he yells out. 'You'll never fucken see her again anyway!'

The men's room door swings open at the far end of the corridor. Goon Zombie stumbles out and starts staggering towards us, his long hair dripping with vomit.

'I have to go, Sophia. Where are my shoes?'

She hands me my shoes, 'You tell me yours.'

'Young.'

'Got it.'

'Okay.'

I chuck on my shoes and chase up to Max. Skatey Driver is manning the 24-hour reception, leaning back in his chair, with his manky skate shoes up on the counter. He stands up all confused as we pass.

'Everything alright with the accommodation, boys?'

Unresponsive.

We run into the cold darkness of the clearing and carry on down the steep, winding gravel driveway and keep running until we get to the main road. And we stop. And all that surrounds us in this moment is darkness and silence, bar our lungs screaming for oxygen in the cold night air.

Chapter 37

Lorne, Part Four

It's stopped snowing and the night sky has cleared. As I always do every time the sky will allow it, I look up to find the Southern Cross. There are a few imposter constellations that look similar, but I can tell the real from the fake once I find it. Closest thing to some sort of centre of this world sometimes. We walk in silence for the first bit. Nausea from the goon grows in my guts. My liver, beaten and bruised, is clearly working overtime to bounce the alcohol from my system, which up to this point, has successfully numbed all sense of self reflection and forethought, though, I'm certain both will return with a vengeance soon. It's coming up four-in-the-morning, and only the light from the stars gives any hint to the weave of the road.

'You reckon we'll get back in time for checkout?' Max asks.

'Fuck if I know,' I say. 'They better not have the cheek to charge us for another fucken night, though.'

'I think that goon may have been past its best. Sat a little rough on the guts.'

'You're welcome by the way,' I say. 'Really. No need to thank me. That's what friends are for, you complete and utter fucken mess.'

'What are you going on about? I was the one who saved your arse.'

'I'll be straight up, speaking open and honestly from the heart, like a man of modern times. There's a good chance I wouldn't have been loitering in the shithouse of a two-star backpackers had it not been for the fact that some cunt in my company can't handle his piss at thirty-fucken-years-old.'

A noise escapes Max that's half a sigh and half a laugh.

'Hey, I've seen you fucked up before. Plenty of times. Remember when my auntie had that party at her place that time?'

'Yes, that was when I was eighteen. But I'm not now. Neither are you, if you hadn't noticed. You need to get your head around that fact pretty fucken quick. Or do you plan to stay like this forever, do you? Teenager forever?'

'This whole fucken weekend was your idea, mate. I didn't ask for it. Wasn't too fussed about the whole ordeal, to tell you the truth. But I thought I'd be a good mate and go along with it all. Help you out with some wingman duties.'

'Nice fucken job you did of that.'

'Would you be so critical of the evening's proceedings if a girl wasn't involved?'

'It's got fuck all to do with that,' I say.

'Everyone sees through you, mate. You ditch us for six years and come back to us acting like you got this life shit down better than all of us. You're as single as me, or Trent, or even Bones cos fuck knows where he's gonna wash up. You don't have it any more worked out than any of us. You need to get your head around that fact pretty fucken quick.'

'Yeah, well, how about we ask that vomit down the front of your hoody, then. I'm pretty certain it would vote me over you right now.'

'Maybe it's done you good to come back to reality. Maybe this is what you needed.'

'What? This?'

I walk in a full circle in the middle of the empty road with my arms outstretched.

'This?' I say. 'This doing me a whole lot of fucken good, you think?'

'You're trying to hustle me for a thank you, when I'm the one putting a fucken roof over your head every fucken night?'

'Remind me to post a thank you card to your folks tomorrow, seeing they funded the fucken project.'

'Fuck, man. I helped you out when you needed it.'

'Yeah, but you said fuck all, didn't you?'

'About what?'

'You know about what.'

'What did you want me to say?'

'It doesn't matter now, does it?'

'What the fuck was I supposed to say, Jackson?'

And it's all piled up on me, it has.

'That she was fucken wrong!' I say. 'That what she did was wrong. That I'm an alright bloke, and I didn't deserve it, and she was a fucken idiot to let me go!'

And I scream, 'Fuck!' as loud as I can to the stars and walk off at full pace to get as far away from Max as I can.

We walk for a while in silence.

Then Max yells out behind me.

'That's the stark truth of the matter, mate. No one needs us now. Not how they used to anyway. Some would prefer the sperm of literal wankers!'

I don't reply. I'm thinking of the hundred fucken corners the courtesy van took from the tavern to the backpackers and how much longer they'll take to walk. Max continues with a raised voice that bounces around the surrounding hills.

'I fell for a girl twice while you were with Chelsea. The first one ditched me for drugs, and the second one broke up with me on my birthday. We'd only been going out for a few months, but still, on my FUCKEN birthday? I half suspect it was in lieu of forken out for a fucken present. And you weren't around to meet either of them, let alone tell me anything I needed to fucken hear.'

Max runs up behind me until he's walking right alongside me. Some dingos he's woken up and stressed out, howl in the distance.

'I don't know what went on between you and Chelsea,' Max says. 'You can tell me if you want, or it's fine if you don't. But I know, mate. I know.'

'I'm fucken over it,' I reply.

'You don't think I could tell how devastated you were that morning you crashed out on my sofa? I took you in without one fucken word of complaint or asking anything in return. I was saying something, you know.'

I'm not replying.

Max goes on.

'I swear to God, mate, this is the first and last time I say anything like this. The way I see it is this: Bad shit will fly at you. But you can't believe it's inherent. You can't. No matter what. You just fucken can't. You got it?'

We climb the hills and valleys in silence. We round corners, walk along long straights, and eventually letterboxes of houses buried deep in the bush begin to appear. And slowly, the letterboxes get closer and closer together, and I start to see a little bit of light on the edge of the sky, and the birds begin their day by screaming bloody murder at each other in the trees. A station wagon with surfboards strapped to its roof drives past us, and the legends give us a toot-toot and chuck a shaka out the window.

They're alright, that lot.

'I've taken a job transfer to Sydney,' I tell Max. 'I move in three weeks.'

Max doesn't say anything. He just looks ahead and we keep on walking. I look over at him a couple of times, but he still keeps looking straight ahead.

We reach the main street of Lorne. Café workers in black aprons are putting out chairs and tables on the footpath, but my guts are still way too raw to stomach the concept of food. In the park, by the beach, right next to our hotel, a small group practices Tai Chi, and I'm intensely jealous of every one of those peaceful, zen'd out fucks. And then he says something, Max does.

'You're a good bloke. She was an idiot to let you go.'

Chapter 38

A Guest

It's Friday night, coming on ten.

'I still don't understand why this is all you have?' she asks.

'What time do you need to get to the airport by?' I ask.

'Seriously, you should treat yourself to some stuff someday.'

'I used to have more than this. This is just a temporary setup, until I get a place of my own. I used to have it all sorted, believe it or not. At my last place, I had a four-poster bed, satin sheets, pillows in pillow cases, lots of cushions everywhere, and piles of towels. Had a whole cupboard full of clean towels. It was quite nice, actually.'

'And where's she now?'

'What time's your flight?'

Max was wrong. I would see Sophia again. She found me and sent a message saying she had a fun night and asked if I'd like to meet up in Melbourne. I extended an invitation for her to stay with me for her final few days before she gaps it back to Heathrow. She accepted the offer because it turned out she had a massive fight with her friends, on the bus from Lorne to Melbourne, and they all decided it was best to go their own ways. She told me she doubts she'll ever speak to them again.

I didn't bother to run this whole scenario past Max. When he got in late the other night, all exhausted from teaching remedial social studies, he saw the two of us snuggled up on his sofa watching *The Sign of our Times with Nigel Lassiter*. I simply told him then and there that Sophia was staying for a few nights. Max didn't have too much to say about it. Went straight to his room and stayed there. But I'm certain it annoyed him a little bit; if not straight up jealousy, then at least a touch pissed off at my overall lack of common courtesy, but I consider it all karma correcting things for his little blowout at the backpackers last weekend; I felt like he owed me a favour for making a mess of himself, and because Max is not often one to take anything upon himself, I had to arrange it all for him.

While I've been at work, wrapping up things before my big move to Sydney, Sophia's been out exploring the city. The weather's been awful to be honest. It more or less rained the whole week. She took lots of pictures of vandalism, though. She sat me down on the sofa and showed me them all. I even pretended to be impressed so she didn't feel bad. I guess you can let the odd opinion slide from time to time. I told her she needs to come back one day and see Melbourne in spring. That's when this town really comes alive, when the trees get their leaves back.

Sophia's wrapping the cord around her hair straightener as she finishes up packing her backpack. I'm inspecting my air mattress, trying to work out where the leak is. I'm having fuck all luck with it, though. Always waits until I'm asleep before it starts shitting air. I guess I've got no other choice but to scrub Max's bath this weekend, fill it up, shove the air mattress in, and try to find some bubbles.

'Do you remember much about your visit to London?' Sophia asks.

'Not really. I was only six at the time. I remember seeing *Jesus Christ Superstar*, though. At the West End. I remember that clearly. Ended up seeing it twice.'

'You're a fan of musical theatre?'

'Took to the story. Went a little manic for the next two weeks. My parents took me back to the Lyceum in their last attempt to calm me down.'

'Did you go to church much when you were younger?'

'Only the once.'

'Do you believe in something else, Jackson? Beyond all this?'

'Dunno. Feels like throwing a dart drunk at a dartboard. There's a fair few fucken theories being thrown around, that's for fucken certain. Everyone's an expert. It's like those articles on life advice written by someone on their death bed. I mean, it's such a skewed and biased perspective that it's almost inapplicable to anyone's everyday life. All that "live every day like it's your last" bullshit. That's why none of us can walk around Max's backyard barefoot. Where's this fucken leak?'

'Well, this is my view of it, seeing you're asking. People know me by different names. My father calls me Petal, you call me Sophia, and my ex calls me Whorish Harlot because he deep dived too far into Freud after we broke up. I'm still the one and the same, though. I only change through other's eyes.'

'So, what do you think there is, then? Other than this?'

'Who knows?' she says. 'All I'm saying is I don't believe anyone should wake up in the middle of the night covered in sweat on account of one scribe's take on things. What about you? Do you think there's something on the other side?'

'I'm open to the concept.'

'Seen a ghost?'

'I just reckon naysayers tend to change their tune pretty fucken quick when death finds someone they know. You rarely hear "worm food" woven into eulogies, do you. It's like in that actual moment, when it finally comes down to it, deep down in their bones, they know.'

'I think you should come to London.'

'For a visit?'

'Or longer.'

'Look, Sophia. You're still on holiday mode. All this you feel here,' I say, whirling my finger in the air at the mouldy ceiling, 'it's not real. Even me. Even though, right now, you absolutely believe it is. You'll fly back home, back to your little life in London, and everything will go back to normal. You'll have your family, and you'll have your friends. You'll get a job, and then you'll run into some hedge fund manager at the polo, pop out a trifecta of kids, then that'll be you. And all I'll be is some guy you met in Australia once.'

'Twice.'

'Semantics.'

'I don't think it could hurt to show yourself a bit of love from time to time, Jackson.'

'Don't even fucken start on that sermon!' I say, louder than I would have liked.

'Settle down,' Sophia says.

'One thing I do know for certain is the whole world's full enough of themselves already. No fucken doubt in my mind about that one there.'

'A lot get that wrong,' she says. 'It's not about standing in front of the bathroom mirror tugging off at your reflection each morning. All it is, is buying yourself some soap. Or a proper bed.'

'This air mattress is only temporary. I'll get a bed when I get a place of my own. I told you that.'

'But so is everything.'

'Well, yeah. My point proved. Sometimes it all feels a fucken waste of time: each one of us spending our days trying to prove that we're somehow different to all the other sacks-of-shit out there.'

'Trust me, Jackson. You're different. It's just hard to get a win with you sometimes.'

She zips up her backpack and jumps on the air mattress, landing on her knees and knocking some more air out of it, which slightly irritates me as now I'm gonna have to blow it up again before we go to bed. I need to remind myself to buy a foot pump with my next pay. And she kisses me, her red hair flowing over my face.

'Are you going to miss me?' she asks.

'Maybe a little bit,' I say.

'At least apply for your visa before you turn thirty. Leave it another year and my lot won't want anything to do with you. All you'll be to us is some sorry old man at the bottom of the earth. No use to anyone at all,' she says with a smile.

'So, I land in London. Then what?'

'Then we'll see what happens from there.'

'See what happens?'

'Let fate decide.'

'Yeah, I don't believe the world works like that anymore.'

'You don't believe what will be, will be?'

'Oh, I believe what will be, will be. That's different to fate, though.'

'You don't think everything happens for a reason?'

'People who say that assume every story has a happy ending.'

'So, what about yours, then? How will yours end, Jackson? Is yours a sad story? Do you not think you deserve happiness?'

'No one deserves anything, any less or any more than anyone else. All I'm saying is London's a long way for a maybe.'

'Everything in life's a maybe. That's life. That's the game. Melbourne's not going anywhere. In a year's time, there'll be three new bars and four new skyscrapers. That's all you'll miss out on. Whatever happens in London—this or that, mays or maybes—at least you'll experience a new city. Or you can stay here and get wasted with Max at dingy backpacker bars every Saturday night. Completely up to you.'

'When does your flight leave?'

'Six A.M.'

'I'll set the alarm for two, then.'

'Do try to not take it all so seriously, Jackson. Be grateful you snuck in. If you'd come along thirty years later, you may well not have made it past the end of your father's sock.'

Chapter 39

The Two Envelopes

Friday. I'm eating my burger at my desk. It's lunchtime, but I'm working through, trying my best to take my mind off thinking. My phone rings. It's an unknown number, so I let it roll through to voicemail for fear of it being a client with a question. A minute later, it rings again. Again, an unknown number. I put down my burger and answer the phone.

'Yeah?'

'It's Blank. Tab's due. Come tonight. Sin Bin. Ten on the dot. Five grand. Brown paper bag. Count it twice.'

And the phone goes dead.

****

I walk into The Sin Bin just before ten. Barry spots me and nods over to a table in the corner where Blank is sitting alone. The only other patrons are the two loose cuts, still playing darts. Blank's dressed slightly more formal than when I first met him. He's wearing a white shirt, a black bow tie, and a green velvet jacket with over-sized lapels. He's retained the black driving gloves, though. I walk over to him, and he stands up and shakes my hand.

'Jackson Donald Young! Welcome, welcome. Sit, sit. Can I shout you a drink?'

'Nah, I'm good, thanks. Try to take things easy on a Friday night. Leave something in the tank for Saturday,' I say, taking my seat.

On the table is an empty whiskey glass, a full jug of iced water, and two envelopes. There's no writing on either envelope. Just a black envelope and a red envelope, lying in the middle of the table.

'Well, I think I will shout myself another drink,' Blank says. 'You sure you don't want one, Jackson? You don't have to buy me back. My shout.'

'No, I'm fine. Thanks, though.'

'Another of the same please, Barry!' Blank yells at the bar, holding up his empty whiskey glass.

'So, what are these, then?' I ask, looking at the envelopes.

'These two? Well, Jackson. Inside these two is the truth you paid for.'

'Why are there two?'

'The black envelope,' he says, tapping it once with his gloved finger, 'this is yours to keep, Jackson.'

And he taps the other.

'Now, the red one? This is yours to read if you choose to. Once. But you can't take it with you. The red envelope never leaves this bar.'

'Why? What's the difference?'

Blank taps the space between the two envelopes.

'You know what this is? This space right here? This is the no man's land of legality. That's why you can't take the red envelope with you. If you did, you'd become a liability, and we can't have that.'

He smiles and taps his temple.

'You'll just have to keep the red one up here.'

I stare at the two envelopes on the table: the black envelope and the red envelope.

'And now all you're thinking is What's in the red envelope? Right?'

Blank pulls the red envelope towards him and puts it down by his side.

'Never mind the red envelope,' he says. 'Often people don't even bother to open the red envelope at all.'

'Why?'

'Variety of reasons. Their own mental sanity, mainly. For many, the black envelope is all their mind can handle. Do you have the money, Jackson?'

I put the brown paper bag on the table.

'You counted it twice?' Blank asks.

'Yes, twice.'

'Good enough for me. Anyway, I know where you live,' he says with a wink. 'Okay, okay, okay. The black envelope. We always start with the black envelope.'

Blank slides the black envelope across the table.

'You're welcome to read it here if you choose, though, some prefer to read it in a private space. Perhaps you'd like to take it into the men's room and lock yourself in a cubicle?'

'It's okay,' I reply. 'Here's okay.'

And I rip open the black envelope.

Chapter 40
Black

Dear Jackson Donald Young

Thank you for your purchase of the following truth. While the content of this truth may not be to your personal enjoyment, please be assured that every step has been taken to verify its accuracy beyond any reasonable doubt.

Your former girlfriend, Chelsea Martin, 29, florist, broke off your relationship as a result of the guilt she was feeling due to a six-month affair she had been participating in with Nigel Lassiter, 56, broadcaster. The affair was most often conducted at your former residence, while you were at work.

Yours sincerely,
Blank.

Chapter 41

Mock the Meat

I'm feeling sick. I keep reading it over and over. Blank sits there in silence sipping his whiskey. I slam the paper down on the table.

'Nigel fucken Lassiter!' I say. 'Out of all the fucken fuckwits in this fucken town!'

Blank's eyes start darting around in every direction other than my own. And all that comes with this answer is more questions. They all stampede through my mind. How did it start? Had she done this before? What day did she lose feelings? But out of all them, the one fucken question that keeps fronting top of mind is What the fuck was Nigel Lassiter's hygiene routine for his filthy dick and sack?

Blank's first to break the silence.

'Look, Jackson. I'm not the best at these types of things,' he says, his eyes returning to mine. 'But there's been a fine man who has sat where you're sitting right now, and there will be a fine man who sits there after you.'

'Six months,' I say, shaking my head. 'Six months it was going on.'

'And now you know. Focus on that, Jackson. Now you know. The worst is the not knowing, right? And that's over now. Now you know.'

'It doesn't feel like I thought it would, though.'

'It rarely does, so I'm told. Now, let me first make this very, very clear. What you are holding in your hand is your truth. You paid for it. It's yours to do with it whatever you wish. However—'

And he stops, as if he's gathering his thoughts.

'However, what?' I ask. 'However, what?'

'However, your particular truth, due to the figure involved, would without doubt fall into the realm of public interest. And if you were willing to sell your truth, I could connect you with a buyer who would pay you 25K for that little black envelope of yours.'

'25K?'

'Look, Jackson. Professionally, I try my best to sit on the fence when it comes to these kinds of things. But you don't owe her any loyalty, mate. Take the 25K, chuck a backpack on your back, and go see the world. Climb Machu Picchu, drink buckets of piss on a beach in Thailand, or go shoot some rhino. That's what I'd do if I was sitting where you're sitting right now. I'd do it in a heartbeat, I swear, if I didn't have a whole lot of other shit to sort out here. That's a winner you're holding there, Jackson. There's no changing the past, but that's a 25K winner you're holding in your hand right now.'

'Then everyone would know.'

'As I said Jackson, this is your truth. No one else's. It's your decision to make and yours alone.'

'Do I have to decide now?'

'To demand an answer at this very time would be an exploitation of an emotional situation for my own personal gain. That's not how I do business, Jackson. Tell you what. If that little black envelope finds its way into those big hairy hands of Barry over there, any time before the year is out, you'll wake up the next day with an extra 25K in your bank account.'

Blank reaches out his hand.

'Your blessing or your curse.'

And we shake.

'So, what about the red envelope?' I ask.

'Ah yes, the red envelope. Now, you can read it if you choose to do so. But I will need you to hand it back to me as soon as you're done. You absolutely cannot take the red one with you. Those are the rules. You understand?'

'Yes, fine,' and I hold out my hand. 'I'm ready.'

'Are you sure you want to do this? Was the black envelope not enough?'

'Yes. I want to know it all. All of it.'

'And you're certainly welcome to it. You paid for it after all. I just sometimes wonder what good comes of these things. But as I said, you paid for it, so it's yours to read.'

Blank lifts the red envelope from his side and slides it across the table.

Chapter 42

Red

Dear Jackson Donald Young

It is imperative that you return this document to the fine gentleman sitting opposite you as soon as you have finished reading its contents. This is to protect the many anonymous associates who risked much to source the following truth for you.

'Handbrake is at her mother's tonight. Meet me at mine after I finish work?'
'I can't. He might decide to come home early.'
'To drink his peppermint tea.'
'Don't be mean.'
'Wouldn't you rather Peter crawl through your window instead?'
'Only if I can have him all to myself.'
'You will soon.'
'When?'
'When I know you're serious.'
'I told you I'm serious. I'm the one who needs to know you're serious.'

'You know it's more complicated for me. You need to be
single first. It'll make this all so much cleaner.'
'I know. I can't keep going on like this.'
'Break it off with him tonight.'
'I need to. I feel so bad for him.'
'Do it.'
'Okay, when he gets home.'
'Message me when it's done, and tomorrow I'll take you to
Never Never Land.'
'Okay.'
'Love you, Tinker Bell X'
'Love you, Peter Pan X'

Please promptly hand this paper back to the fine gentleman
sitting opposite you.

Yours sincerely,
Blank.

Chapter 43
Gross Stereopsis

'You're done, yes?' Blank asks.

I look up, and he grabs the piece of paper out of my hand, pulls out a cigarette lighter from the inside pocket of his velvet jacket, and sets it on fire. He waves it violently as the flames crawl up the paper and lick at his black driving gloves. He keeps hold of it until it becomes ash in his hand, then he drops it on the table and pours the big jug of iced water all over it, turning it into a sloppy, ashy mess that drips off the side of the table.

'Tea towel, Barry! Had a spill over here,' Blank yells at the bar, then turns back to me. 'As I said, Jackson, some of these things I do, well, some stray further from the letter of the law than others.'

'Peter fucken Pan!' I say, slamming my fist hard on the table.

'All I ask,' Blank says, 'is that whatever you're thinking, or whatever you're feeling, you go straight home tonight and sleep on it. I know of a few situations where someone sitting in that chair you're sitting in right now, well, they've acted rather impulsively, and it's resulted in—let's call it: long term complications. I'm not saying this out of fear for myself. Not at all. If you go lose your mind and do something stupid, and the police come asking questions at the bar, Barry over there will tell them I'm nothing more than a figment of your fucken imagination, and you'll be laying your shaved head down on the floor of a padded cell every night for the rest of your life. Either way, Jackson, my conscience is clear because all I do is deliver the truth. As I said to you the night we met, it exists. All I do, is find it for whoever wants it.'

'What now, then?'

'Jackson, it's been a pleasure doing business with you,' and he reaches his out his hand, and we shake again. 'Now you know everything you need to know. What you do from here is up to you, and whatever path you choose, I do wish you all the best on your journey. Alas, I must now bid you a fond farewell. Goodbye, Jackson.'

'Bye, Blank. Thanks for all this.'

'Don't mention it,' and Blank calls out to the bar. 'And Barry, a fuck you to you too!'

Blank winks at me and walks out of the bar, seeping back into suburbia.

****

As I walk back to Max's joint through the cold, empty streets, all my memories of her begin to shatter. Long brunches, overseas holidays, movie nights, beach days, bush walks, dinners out, nights in, sleep ins. Each memory, one by one, becomes a chard that cuts its way from the inside out. That feeling, that doubt I always told myself was of my own mind's making, has now been proven to be the truth. Six years. Nothing more than a fantasy I convinced myself to be true. My greatest fear has been realised. That the world *is* how I see it when I'm hungover. Life is nothing more than a list of chores and obligations that I must achieve before nightfall. And nothing more. Until death do I part. I realise now—with full clarity—that how I look in the mirror when I'm hungover, must be how I look to the rest of the world every day. And our holidays and happy moments, they're all just a temporary construct to distract us momentarily from the inevitable pain and hurt that will chase us down and find us all, no matter how fast or how far we try to run from it.

I get back to my bedroom and burrow into my sleeping bag, pulling it over my head for protection. I crave sleep more than anything in the world right now. Not because I'm tired, but because I want to stop my mind from all this thinking. I want my thoughts to stop. To sleep. Goodnight, Jackson. Sleep tight, Jackson. Sweet dreams, Jackson. Peter fucken Pan!

Chapter 44

The Fourth Wall

Chelsea's story ends today. It's coming on nine, Saturday morning. I'm sitting in the middle of the sofa, alone. I'm drinking one of Max's beers for breakfast to calm the nerves. I got out of bed early for this. Not that I was sleeping. No. I've been thinking long and hard about this the entire night. I've looked at this situation from many, many angles and—right or wrong—this is the way it has to be. The thing is with these types, the ones that come at you, they always give you an in. No matter what, they always slip up and give you an in. They always fucken do because they convince themselves they're smarter than everyone else. They're so completely deceived by their own charade that they never see you coming.

Max is still asleep, and I doubt he'll be up before midday anyway. He sleeps in more and more now. And the opening credits roll, *The Word on the Street with Nigel Lassiter.*

'I'm here on Swanston Street, on the steps of the State Library, where last Saturday's peaceful protest was again turned violent by the police. Now, some state officials are petitioning for a blanket ban on inner city demonstrations—'

And I grab Max's car keys from the kitchen counter, and I'm straight out the front door.

****

Max is gonna have some speeding tickets in the post, that's for fucken certain. His old Ibiza shook hard all the way to the State Library, where I parked it in the closest loading zone I could find.

It's a beautiful winter's morning, not-a-cloud-in-the-sky, but it's cold enough that every cunt's still in a coat. I push through the hordes to get a look at Nigel Lassiter. He's standing on the steps of the library, under the big bronze statue of Sir Redmond Barry, surrounded by a mob, some pigeons, and a cameraman. He's waltzing around, shoulders back, chest out, waving his microphone all over the place.

'Sir,' Nigel asks an elderly man. 'How do you feel about the rumoured government proposal to indefinitely ban protest movements on Swanston Street?'

'Dreadful,' the old git replies. 'Though, it would ease congestion, wouldn't it?'

'Shades of complexity to every problem,' Nigel says. 'And you, Ma'am?'

He holds his microphone at some forty-something mum holding her baby.

'Well, I just think that everyone should always be kind to each other, and then no one would need to protest anything.'

'Never a greater truth spoken,' Nigel says.

And he chucks the microphone right up in my face.

'Your thoughts on the matter, mate?'

And I stare him right in the eye.

'All you cunts are living in fucken Never Never Land, as far as I'm concerned.'

He shoves me in the chest and pushes me out of shot.

'Apologies for the language, people,' he says.

Keep thinking you're running the show, mate. You keep thinking that.

Chapter 45
Mutatis Mutandis

Pan hands his microphone to his camera man and takes out his phone from the inside pocket of his black winter long coat. He reads a message, then smiles to himself, and he walks off towards La Trobe Street. And I follow him. He walks past the corner of La Trobe and Russell. And I follow him. Then he goes into a florist. And I wait for him. He's in there for about ten minutes, and then he walks out with a big bunch of flowers. Pink roses. He continues up La Trobe Street. And I follow him. He crosses the intersection and walks into Carlton Gardens. He walks up the path towards the Royal Exhibition Centre, past the big fountain with the nude nymphs spitting water, past the Melbourne Museum, and towards a playground. Pan hands his wife the bunch of pink roses, and she hands him his son. He gives his son a big kiss on the cheek and takes him over to a set of swings and puts him in one of those little swings they have for the little kids, with little holes for their little legs to stick through. He gives his son a gentle push while his wife rubs his back. She leans up and gives him a kiss on the cheek, and I yell out at the fuck.

'Nigel! I have information on Chelsea Martin!'

Unresponsive.

228

And the fact the cunt heard every single word and hasn't looked over, tells me Blank was true to his word. His wife is looking over, though. She's looking over at me all confused. And I go at him again.

'Chelsea Martin! I know the truth about her!'

Pan whispers in the ear of his wife and walks over to me. He grabs my arm and tries to lead me away from the playground.

'What is it you want, mate?' he asks.

I rip my arm from his grip.

'You worked out who I am yet?' I ask.

'I'm guessing you're Jackson.'

'Well done,' I spit. 'That is exactly who I am.'

'So, what are you here to do? Start a punch up in a playground? Over some girl?'

'No. That is not what I am here to do.'

'You need to take a big breath and calm down, mate. Think this through rationally. We were all born with free will. When you come to realise there's no prize on the other side, you'll stop getting so hung up on this concept of the one. Stop letting your ego run the—'

'Shut the fuck up, cunt. I'm the one with the ear of the table now. I know about her, and all the others, and I know about everything you get up to in airport hotels.'

His eyes take me seriously when he hears airport hotels.

'What is it you want, then? An apology? You want me to step aside so you can win your girl back?'

'No. That is not what I want.'

'My advice? Get over her. Jump on any tram in this city. You'll see ten as good as her and five better. You should thank me for a life lesson learnt. A head can be on the pillow next to you, and you'll still know fuck all of what's going on in their mind.'

'Listen to me, cunt. This is how it will fucken work. And listen fucken close because you will not want to fuck this up. Trust me, you won't. When you're done playing with your little son over there, you'll send a message to Chelsea breaking it off. You'll tell her, in as few words as possible, that you're choosing to stay with your wife and son. She'll reply, but you won't. You won't ever fucken reply to her, got it? Never ever will you reply to her.'

Pan turns and looks back at his family. His wife is pushing the tiny little guy in the swing, but she keeps looking over at us all concerned.

'What you need to understand, Pan, is this: I have eyes and ears fucken everywhere. And if I find out you have done anything other than what I have asked, I swear to fucken God, I'll tear off your whole fucken façade.'

'Are you threatening me?

'Yes. That is what I'm doing. I am threatening you. Do I need to make myself any clearer?'

'No,' he says, his eyes still on his wife and son.

'Look at me and tell me you've got it,' I say.

Pan turns and looks at me, 'Yes. I've got it.'

'Here's the truth of the matter, you fucken ranga cunt. You wouldn't last one minute on the forest floor. Not one fucken minute. Now piss off over there and go give your kid a push in the swing, you fucken arsehole.'

I turn and walk away. I'm not looking back. I'm over it all. I wasn't certain about the airport hotels, but at the same time I was. I can read it in their eyes now—the airport hotel types. That poor little guy in the swing will one day realise his dad's nothing more than a sack-of-shit. But he needs not to know that now.

Chapter 46

Soma

Two weeks ago, a couple of cops found a white Mercedes with its bonnet wrapped around a lamppost, a few doors down from a brothel in Brighton. The air bags were deployed, and there was blond hair and blood stuck to the roof of the passenger's side. Both front doors were wide open, but no one was inside. The cops phoned in the plates to head office, and it turned out they belonged to one Richard Fitzpatrick. Later that night, when the cops kicked in Rick's front door to ask him about his whereabouts earlier that evening, Rick straight-batted them with claims that junkies jacked his car. But the cops weren't fucken idiots. Eventually, Rick broke down crying. My boss told me that Rick's wife got a little upset about it all too. Rick never came back to work. Turns out Richard Fitzpatrick has enough skeletons in his closet to fill Coburg cemetery ten times over, once he got all confessional with the cops over tea and biscuits. Now he's living at some Yarra Valley health retreat, tending to a small flock of sheep, making reusable woolen tampons for women in third world countries while working through a few personal issues. My boss reckons it's mostly so it'll all look a little bit better when they wheel him out in front of the magistrate next month.

Anyway, that's why Rick's not here at my leaving drinks. It's been a couple of interesting weeks, that's for sure. It's Friday night, and I've chosen to have my going away drinks at Gin Den because it's chill and it doesn't take too long to get a drink. My boss hands me an envelope and I open it. It's a card with some nice messages and a $25 pre-paid credit card.

'You can put it towards either a holiday in Bora Bora or a new jet ski,' Will whispers to me.

I'm pretty certain he's taking the piss. I sure fucken hope he is anyway. My boss has a spring in his step tonight. He's been going on and on about how much progress he's been making at the gym, but he still looks all the same to my eye. He's also harping on about how our company should do this kind of stuff more often. He even threw out 'every Friday' as an option. Suggested they form some sort of social committee to build morale. Some shit like that. Thankfully, most of his talk regarding this matter is directed at Dita.

I say it's been an interesting couple of weeks because late last Thursday my piss started burning really bad. I needed to keep going to the men's room more and more. Every time I returned to my desk, I needed to get straight back up and go for a piss again, and every time I did, it hurt more and more. It felt akin to pissing out glass with a piece of rusty barbed wire pegged down my shaft. It was getting fucken embarrassing, to be honest. Will and Dita pretended not to notice how often I was going, but, of course, they did. Always looked up when I got up and never looked up when I sat back down. I searched phrases like 'venereal disease' and 'incubation periods' and 'home remedies.' In my lunch break, I bought a two-litre bottle of cranberry juice from the 7-Eleven on Swanston and sculled the whole thing right there at the counter. Did fuck all for the pain, though. In the end, I realised I had no other option but to phone the situation in to a medical professional. But there was no fucken way I was going to put a matter as important as this, in the hands of some neophyte at some shopping plaza medical centre. So, I called in sick Monday morning and caught the number 1 tram back to Albert Park to see our old family doctor. The gap used up the last of my pay, but sometimes you just need to throw some money at a situation, and this was one of those times. My doctor, though, she did a really good job of acting like it was no big deal at all. Told me to hide behind the curtain and piss in a jar, and that it'd take a couple of days to get the results back, and then she'd know exactly what I had, and from there she could work out the specific antibiotics I needed to get it all cleared up. I told her I was in a lot of fucken pain, and I asked her if there was anything she could give me on the spot to make it all stop. She told me: no. Told me that I'd have to put up with it until she got the test results back from the lab. Yesterday morning at work, I received a message from her.

'All clear, mate.'

Anyway, my piss stopped burning straight away, and I stopped needing to go so often after that.

Chapter 47

Pay Day

I wake up to my phone alarm going off under my pillow. It's set to five-in-the-morning. Today is Tuesday. I also wake up to another sore back courtesy of the flimsy mesh wire that's holding up the thin mattress of my bottom bunk. It's better than what I had previously, though. Took me nearly three weeks to finally secure this prime bottom bunk real estate. It was a full-on fucken fistfight to get it, that's for fucken certain. Had to throw some Norwegian cunt against the lockers when he tried to snake me for the bottom bunk after the Chinese girl who had previously held the deed moved on to Byron Bay.

I grab my towel that's still drying on the ladder of the bunk above me, which for the last three nights has been occupied by a French Canadian called Francois who has a horrific case of sleep apnea. Very quietly—so as not to disturb the sleeping and the coma'd—I open my locker and take out my suit, my pre-ironed shirt, and my tie, all hanging up neatly inside.

I walk down the hallway to the communal showers. I pull back the curtain of the first shower stall and see that someone has had a massive chuck during the night because there's vomit all caught up in that plastic grippy thing that's supposed to stop you from slipping over. But all this scatological stuff fails to faze me now. I simply walk to the next stall and try my luck again. This one looks to be as clean as one can hope for in accommodation such as this, aside from a generous serving of pubic hair clogging up the plug hole.

At the basin, I brush my teeth. In the mirror, I tweak my half-Windsor until it's sitting perfectly straight. Appearance is everything in my line of work. I walk downstairs to the communal kitchen and time it perfectly for the start of the continental breakfast that comes complimentary when you stay three nights or more. This morning, I've decided on a bowl of rice bubbles with a side of vegemite on toast. Like most mornings for the last several weeks I eat alone, as there is seldom anyone up at this early hour. And even on the rare occasion there is, say for a day trip to the Blue Mountains, the corporate attire I wear to the breakfast table confuses most of the other backpackers to the point of avoidance. I think everyone here considers me a little odd because I tell them I choose to live semi-permanently at this backpackers because I love communal living and the entire concept of other people in general. As soon as I'm done with my breakfast, which should get me through to my Big Man Stew in a Can tonight, I step outside into another beautiful Sydney morning. Bright shards of sun are starting to slice up the long shadows from the night just gone. I slip into the current of pedestrian commuters making their way down George Street. It's a warm morning, so my suit jacket is tucked under my arm. It's got an alright climate this town, I'll give it that. My jacket would go straight in the bin if it wasn't for our CEO James having recently made it compulsory to wear one to all face-to-face client meetings.

I received a phone call at work from Will the other day. A postcard from Belarus arrived for me at the Melbourne office.

Will wanted to know if he should redirect it up to our Sydney office, and I told him to just read it down the phone and save some poor postman cunt all the hassle.

> Hey Jackson,
> Ditched the folks once my arse was good enough to
> fly. Missed my son a bit. Come visit if you're ever in
> this neck of the woods. First lappy dance on me.
> Bones.

I asked Will how it was going down in Melbourne. He said it had all gone a bit downhill since I left. A couple of weeks back, Carl sat Will and Dita down at the boardroom table and made them watch a three-hour video of some patronising spectacled cunt explaining to them everything that was wrong with our generation. Dita went out for lunch that day and never came back. Turns out her timing couldn't have been any worse because it was the same week Carl had to take a whole lot of time off work to front court for his custody battle. So, my boss made Will head the Cockburn presentation one-up. Didn't go too well by the sounds of it. Will said he had to take the next two weeks off work to recover, you know, just to get his head back in the right place. I told him he shouldn't worry about it too much. Will said he's thinking of moving to Canada to wax skis.

I sit down at my desk and fire up my computer. I really am a new man in Sydney. I doubt anyone from the Melbourne office would even recognise me now. I'm a complete picture of professionalism. I've also become a big believer in the early bird. 'Get me some fucken early worms to eat,' I like to say now. I'm at my desk every morning before seven. Without fail.

Even beat our CEO James into work most mornings. He thinks I'm a star, he does. Because, as he always says, you get out what you put in. And he's right. The results speak for themselves. I've absolutely smashed my September budget, and my October forecast predicts a record month for me. Last Monday, in our general sales meeting, I got a rapturous round of applause from the entire boardroom table. Our CEO James called me, 'a fucken supers'ar.'

James, for the record, is some alcoholic English arsehole who seemingly swindled an entire board of directors for the gig with nothing more than an offshore accent that wants fuck all to do with the letter T. That, and a shameless willingness to go for cheap laughs through curse words. I laugh the loudest at the boardroom table when he does that, when the lazy cunt swears for cheap laughs. I think that's why he's taken such a shine to me so quickly. I've been told CEO James and our 2IC Emma bang bits in the stationery cupboard afterhours. Like him, she's married. Mother to two beautiful boys. Sometimes the sheer fucken predictability of it all, is just as offensive as the rest of it.

I've told all my workmates that I've signed a short-term lease on an apartment at the top of George Street. It's only temporary, until I get settled into Sydney life. I'm genuinely considering buying when the market finally settles. I can see myself living here for good, I really can. Sunny Sydney. When someone asks me how my weekend was, in the torturous lift ride up to the forty-fourth floor, I tell them I spent both days attending open homes and auctions, just to get a feel of what the market is doing right now.

A couple of weeks back, we had this big Friday night work drinks at some bar down by the Opera House. Compulsory waterboarding to celebrate our team hitting our third-quarter sales incentive. It was also a good chance for us to get to know each other, to come closer as a team. But after they held me down and made me scull a pint of piss coffee, I faked a death in the family and ordered a ride back to the backpackers. Spent the rest of the night in the little bar they've got going on in the basement, getting wasted alone on jugs of their Pirate Bitter. The last thing I wanted was to feel part of that team, to sense even the slightest attachment to any of it, to blur the lines of my own reality, for fear that I might wake in my bunk one morning firmly believing my own bullshit.

****

It's four-in-the-afternoon, and some short runt two desks over jumps out of his pants all fucken excited. Fist pumping and high fives, all that carry on. I've got no idea what his name is, nor most of the others. To be perfectly honest, I can't be arsed with the effort required to commit the names of these fascist fucks to memory. Short Runt will more than suffice for the short term.

'Got fucken paid, we did!' Short Runt screams, jumping up and down on his chair.

This is it. This is fucken it. I log in to my bank account, and Short Runt's correct. It's there. All off it. My base, my commission, my bonus, and my 25K relocation reimbursement.

'Anyone fancy a coffee?' I ask the office. 'My shout. Pay day!'

And every cunt puts their hand up. Even our CEO James barks his order from his office, so I have to run around with a fucken pen and paper taking a full order of long blacks, flat whites, lattes, no sugar, soy fuck, almond shit, and a green smoothie with a spirulina booster—which isn't even a fucken coffee. I return to my desk and open the top drawer with the tiny key I've been wearing around my neck since the day I started here. From the back of the drawer, I take out my leather travel wallet. I open it, just to be certain they're both still there. They are. My passport and the black envelope. This is it. This is fucken it. And I freeze for a moment. I stare at the leather travel wallet in my hand. This is it. This is it. And I look around at all the others. Their heads buried in their keyboards. The walls aren't real. The walls aren't real. The walls aren't real. And I tuck in my seat and tell everyone I'll be back soon with their coffees and smoothie. And I calmly walk through the frosted doors with the company logo, leaving my suit jacket hanging on the back of my chair.

Chapter 48

Wanderlust

I'm walking fast up George Street, heading back to the backpackers, weaving in and out of the slow-walking who clearly have way too much time on their hands today. Thunder thighs swinging violently from side-to-side but still getting nowhere fast. As I'm walking, I'm running through my evacuation plan one final time. I've rehearsed this in my head every day since Carl first offered me the transfer to Sydney.

This will be an in/out job.

I return to my dorm and strip off my suit pants, my shirt, and my tie. I kick off my school shoes and cram the whole lot of it into the tiny rubbish bin next to the lockers. I change into cuffed black pants, a white T-shirt, and bright blue casual kicks, and I drag my backpack out of my locker where it's been sitting in wait for the last eight weeks, meticulously packed with all the essentials for long-term travel. A hungover girl is still in bed. Louise is her name, from Ireland. She sits up and brushes her messy blond hair out of her face.

'Leaving us, Ed?' she asks.

'Yep.'

'Where you going?'

'The airport.'

'Where to after that?'

'Cross that bridge when I come to it,' and I put my arm through each strap of my backpack and hoist it onto my back.

'Enjoy Australia.'

I chuck my room card at some cunt on reception and walk up George Street, cross over to Elizabeth, past Hyde Park, all the way up to Central Station where I jump on the next train to Sydney Airport.

****

I'm standing under the departures sign. It's a weird sensation: knowing I can go anywhere I want to. I walk around a bit, until I find the airport travel agent. I stand there staring at all the different destinations they have up on their O-mazing October specials board. After a while, the lady behind the desk invites me to take a seat. She tells me it's not the cheapest way to buy flights, buying them last minute at the airport, but she'll do the best she can for me. I tell her that's fine. I tell her that I expected that to be the case. But I figure, in a sense, work's paying for it, so I'm not too worried about paying overs. I tell her that I need to find a cheap country to park up in for a bit. Somewhere to hang out and stretch the coin as far as possible. Some place where I don't have to think too far beyond the next beer. I tell her I'm torn between Asia and South America. I'm taking Eastern Europe off the table altogether. I tell her that I want fuck all to do with back-to-back winters like Bones has to do. If there's ever a sign that you've fucked up somewhere along the line of life, it's when you cop back-to-back winters. This travel agent, though, she's very helpful. She tells me Thailand will be the cheapest to get to, but I can only stay there for thirty days without a visa. I can travel to Argentina visa-free for up to ninety days on a one-way ticket. Colombia's the same but requires evidence of onward travel. Same goes for Peru and Brazil. Venezuela's working through a few personal issues at present, and Chile's immigration page was way too confusing for either of us to get our heads around. So, I decide on Argentina. I know fuck all about that part of the world, apart from this movie they made us watch in primary school about a plane full of Uruguayans who crashed into the side of the Andes and ended up eating each other.

I check in my backpack at the Air New Zealand terminal and start walking towards the departure gate. My flight leaves in an hour. They're making me do a stopover in fucken Auckland, though. Jesus Christ. Last time I set foot in that fucken dystopia was when me and my mates went there for New Year's once. That's going way back, right after we finished school. A story and a half, that trip was. I'll take a plane crash and cannibalism over a repeat of that experience any day.

I'm reading through the itinerary that my travel agent printed out for me. The flight from Auckland to Buenos Aires is a fair fucken hike, but total travel time is not something I'm overly concerned about right now. My top priority is not hanging around here for one fucken minute longer than I have to. I'm more than fucken done with it all. More than fucken done.

****

I clear security, customs, and explosives with little fuss, so it leaves me with a bit of time to kill before boarding commences. I find an airport bar and park up on a stool at the end of the bar. At the other end, is some loved-up couple sharing a pizza splattered with rocket and prosciutto. They keep taking lots of pictures of themselves. Sure as shit, they're about to go off travelling the world together on some big long adventure. And for the first time, I feel at peace with the fact that their lot is not for me. Chelsea used to go on and on and on about fernweh. For the monolingual, it's a German word with no direct English translation but more-or-less means feeling homesick for a place you've never even fucken been to. Fucken hell, when those Sauerkrauts get going.... Anyway, the truth is, there's nothing in this world I miss anymore. You keep comparing today to an imaginary tomorrow or a glorified past, and you're never going to be happy in the moment. Get drunk, wake up hungover, and if the sun gets up too, and you can tolerate what the mirror chucks back at you in the morning, that's the best you can hope for really. My next pages are blank. I'll do what I want to, when I want to do it. I'll change my plans with the wind. I'll find love and leave it first. I'll be accused by many of having a fear of commitment. I'll be called a man child or, if I'm really lucky, a fuck boy. I'll be debated and deconstructed around brunches with all her fucken friends who hated me and were right about me all along. No one will get me or understand me because I'll never let anyone close to me, never let anyone in, for fear of becoming a doomed passenger in their life once again. A guillotine can do fuck all if your neck's not in the lunette. I will always do what's right for me. I'll leave before I get hurt, even though I know I will be hurting them first. But I survived and so will they. In time, I'll be so accustomed to my own company that I'll become institutionalised in a self-sufficient existence, and the very notion of sharing my life with someone, to compromise my own happiness, to even consider putting someone else's wants and needs next to my own, let alone before, will come to be considered by myself as incomprehensible. This is my fate. The beer in my hand tastes the best it's ever tasted, and there's nothing quite like the feeling of being at an airport bar, taking in that glorious aroma of aviation fuel, with your entire future ahead of you.

> And you're at the dental hygienist
> They ask you to fill out a form
> It asks, 'How did you hear about us?'
> You write down, 'The brothel receptionist.'

And I'm running back through the terminal, through all the piss and fragrance stores, weaving in and out of the opposing tide of passengers coming the normal way. I stop at the customs counter and start yelling at the two cunts standing behind it. I tell them that I need to come back through. They tell me I can't. They tell me I've already left Australia. I tell them that's fucken ridiculous. A couple of tooled-up airport police strut over to see what all the fuss is about. I tell them I need to speak with my travel agent immediately. One of them shakes his head, and the other starts reading me the riot act.

'Mate, you've already left the country,' he says. 'Once you've passed passport control, you're done. Unless there's been a death in your family, you're going where your fucken ticket says you're going.'

'So, tell me this, mate,' I say. 'If I go destroy a toilet bowl in that men's room over there, what country am I shitting in, then? Tell me that.'

'International waters.'

'I reckon a couple of cylinders have blown out upstairs, mate!' I yell at him.

'Well, here's a little titbit for ya, cunt. Outside of the shitters, Commonwealth law still applies till the plane door is shut. So, if you keep this lip up, and it's a bathroom you need, we've got a nice little one over at our lockup that you're more than welcome to use. You'll have to fight your corpulent French cellmate for your share of the shitter, though. You know what we've nicknamed him after last night's antics? Bidet!'

'Fine,' I say. 'I'll take my fucken flight, then. Save all this fucken melodrama.'

'Paging, Mr Jackson Young. This is your final boarding call for Air New Zealand Flight NZ108 to Auckland. If you are in the terminal, please make yourself known to ground staff at Gate 48 immediately.'

And I'm running back through all the piss and fragrance stores trying to find Gate 48.

'Interested in duty free today, Sir?'

'Go fuck yourself.'

After I work out where I need to be, I run up to Gate 48. At the counter, a lady wearing a purple scarf asks me for my boarding pass and my passport open at the photo page. She says it all in a pissed-off tone, though, and tells me I'm late and holding up the plane. She rips off my boarding pass stub and hands the rest of it back to me and tells me I need to run down the gangway to get there before the cabin door closes.

'Wait,' I say. 'There's one more thing I need to do.'

I take out my phone.

Twenty unread messages.

Nineteen missed calls.

'Sir, I need you to go to the plane. Now!'

'Yes, one moment.'

'Mr Young, they're about to close the cabin doors.'

'Yes, yes, fuck, you're distracting me. I can't fucken focus on two things at once, can I?'

I quickly write out my message to Chelsea.

'Farewell, Tinker Bell.'

I stare at them.

My final two words to her.

I stare at them some more.

'Farewell, Tinker Bell.'

And I delete them. She doesn't deserve that, Chelsea doesn't. The benefit of my insight. So, I withhold that courtesy and hand my phone to the lady behind the counter.

'Can you chuck this in your bin for me?'

'Um, okay.'

And I run down the gangway, reveling in the art of not-knowing.

Chapter 49

Solstice

Tomorrow is the shortest day of the year. It's Friday—gloomy as hell and starting to spit. Not even four-in-the-afternoon and there's no light left in the sky. What a fucken place to live. All the red double decker buses are stuck in traffic because a bit further up some English are protesting America again. I've figured out it's often quicker to walk in this town. The underground is too claustrophobic for my liking. I reckon they built it too deep into the ground. By the time you walk down the stairs, and walk back up the stairs, you might as well have walked there overground, as far as I'm concerned. I'm not sure this city was made for me, but I am where I am. I'm walking down Whitechapel Street, and it's all so busy with so many different faces walking past, all wrapped in winter coats, hoods tied tight.

Twisty-turvy streets all over the joint.

Earlier today, even with the slightest hint of light in the sky, it was way too cloudy for me to find my bearings. Couldn't see the tall buildings to tell me where I was. So, I got a little lost and turned up an hour late for my job interview. Seems that with the weather here, there's little point in looking up. Explains why everyone walks around town with their heads down all the time. It's a pretty complicated city to get your head around, that's for certain. I always end up confused about which side of the river I'm on. Speaking of which, the Thames makes the Yarra look like a Vanuatuan lagoon. Just this morning, I spotted a body floating face down in it. I leaned over the railing and watched it go right under Tower Bridge, and everyone seemed to keep going about their business as if it was no big deal at all. In the end, I found a couple of those bobby blokes walking their beat and mentioned it to them in passing, in case they felt in the mood for a bit of fishing later.

My job interview went terrible anyway, so it doesn't matter now that I was late. That's what I'm walking back from now. It was pretty much my last stab at things before everyone shuts up shop for Christmas. Some pompous bloke on the panel made some curt comment about my lack of references, questioning why I put Will down as my primary referee. Turns out they actually called him. Will was off his face on magic mushrooms at some Canadian ski resort, going hard at it with all the other waxers he's working with. They told me the phone ended up being passed around the party and some colourful language was exchanged. I don't blame Will for that, though. He's alright, Will is. I guess next time I should probably give him the heads-up first. Still, at the time, in the job interview, I wanted to uppercut that mouthy aristocratic cunt and send his lower jaw straight through his stiff upper lip. But instead, I smiled, apologised for Will, and told him there's one more name I can give him.

I'm walking down White Chapel Road, but I'm in no real hurry to get back to the apartment. So, I've decided to go for a bit of an explore. I find this old pub on this old corner, called The Ten Bells. It's right across the street from this old white church. I order a pint of Camden Hells Lager from this pale bartender bloke who tells me he's from Cape Town, and we talk rugby union for a bit. I ask him why the bar is called The Ten Bells, and he tells me it's because the old white church across the street has ten bells.

This place is packed already. Most seem to be going hard at it too. There'll be some rough faces in mirrors tomorrow morning, that's for certain. Everyone here looks like they've got enough friends already, though. Groups of girls and guys, all hanging out together like it's no big deal at all. So, I take a stool at the end of the bar and sit by myself with my beer as company.

I didn't make it to the funeral, Trent's funeral. Max told me as much as he knew. They'd been drinking at Max's joint, the Saturday before last, and Trent got pissed off with Max for not wanting to go out. So, he left. Max reckoned Trent must have thought he was going to miss his train or something and tried to take a shortcut across the tracks. He should never have done that. Trent and his fucken shortcuts. Everyone always in a hurry to get home. Another train would have come along eventually. If only he'd waited. I thought about going back for Trent's funeral. I thought about it hard, but I think I need to bunker down here if things are to work themselves out. In the end, I donated the full cost of a flight home to a charity in Trent's name. It's this sanctuary out Healesville way that looks after birds they find on the edge of the highway. Ones with broken wings and bent beaks and all that. Parrots, hawks, and penguins, they fix them up until they can fly and swim again. I think he would have liked that, Trent would have. Preferred it to my company, at least. I asked Max if he was okay, and he told me he was fine. I said he should come over here for a holiday next summer. He could crash on the sofa, and we could go to Wimbledon. He told me he'd think about it. He said that first he needs to save some coin to build a fence tall enough that the junkies can't throw their needles into his backyard anymore.

He should have never done that, what he did. Trent. Ran for the train. But he did it. I hope I get to see him again sometime. I think he'd be nicer, you know, without all the worry.

Chapter 50

The End

The one thing I will give this town is they maintain their architecture. This apartment is a couple of centuries old, but the caretaker has really kept on top of things. I'd be lying if I called it spacious, but I guess it's doing the job for the meantime. Sophia's grandparents own it, so they give her a fair deal with the rent. It's nice and central and looks over a cute little park right beside the Thames. I've been told it might snow in a couple of days which would be nice. I only stayed for two pints at The Ten Bells before I walked all the way back here. Doesn't matter what bar you're at in this world, other's eyes will let you do one pint on your own, but they start to look at you strange if you do two alone. So, I left. It started to rain down hard on my way home, and all I could see were black and white polka dot umbrellas everywhere. Took me nearly two hours to walk all the way back here. Got to walk past the gates of Buckingham Palace, though. Stuck my head right between the pikes and had a good old look at it all. My God, she was handed a mess to clean up. You've got to admire her for that.

***

It's raining even harder now. The wind's blowing it all up against the windows. Beside one of them is our Christmas Tree. We put it up yesterday. We decorated it with some nice little lights and put a star on the top for Trent. The Christmas Tree's not that big because we don't have much space, but it's a real one—that's the main thing. Gives the whole apartment that nice Christmas Tree smell. My phone hums in my pocket. I pull it out and it's a message from Sophia.

'Hey, sorry. Work drinks carrying on a bit. Might be late.'

I don't reply. I just sit in my red chair, sip my peppermint tea, and start to think about things. I think of Barry the Bartender, and I think of Blank. I imagine Barry would be replacing all the stolen urinal cakes in the men's room about now. I give him a call.

'Sin Bin. Barry speaking.'

It only takes a moment
To fear
What you know you've become

'Hello?'

Hello?

And I hang up. It has to end here. It has to. I think of everything that has passed, and I think of everyone. I think of them all. And I think of Chelsea. And for the first time since the first night I met her, I think of Chelsea and feel nothing. She, no doubt, would tell this all another way, but I did what I had to do.

THE END

***

I hear keys rattle in the front door. It swings open, and Sophia walks in with a dripping wet black and white polka dot umbrella. She takes off her red tartan coat, pulls her black beanie from her red hair, and starts undoing the laces of her black boots.

'Home, finally,' she sighs.

And she smiles as she walks across the room and sits down on my lap. And she runs her hands through my hair and kisses me hard. You know, as if she likes me.

Raz Andrews VIR List

Thirsty for more?

Follow the link below to add yourself to the Raz Andrews VIR List. You'll receive the free visual companion booklet, *Maps of Malicious Mates*, and you'll be straight to the front of the line when it comes to new releases and exclusive reader opportunities.

Join now at razandrews.com.

Please Leave a Review

Reviews help other readers find great books. Raz Andrews encourages you to share your thoughts on *Malicious Mates* at your preferred book seller.

About the Author

RAZ ANDREWS was born in the eighties and raised in Takapuna, New Zealand. He currently lives in Melbourne, Australia. *Malicious Mates* is his debut novel. You can find him online at razandrews.com.

Acknowledgements

Thanks to Geoffrey Andrews, Phyllis Andrews, Nola Andrews, Christina Andrews, Jacques Hopkins, Margaret Hopkins, Sarah Trounson, Andrew Trounson, George Paradise, Matthew Cridge, Brittany Nolan, S. Bioletti, Jacques LeBoozé, Sammo XCX, Late Night Kerr, The Fuck Ox, Big Sleazy, The Hammer, Hardo, Ngom de Plume, Sticky Stick, The Walligator, Hemming Lövgren, Marianne Lövgren, Azza Raveendran, Hugh Cox, Paul Crowley, Mike De Napoli, Brad Fitzgerald, Vince Gilligan, James Napier Robertson, Paula Panopoulos, Pawel Kardis, Zahid Gamieldien, Yasmin Khan, Kelly Rigby, Pia Riley, Nina Ariana, Jake Arnott, Mike Baranik, Gairden Cooke, Anna Davis, Alex Edmonds, Paul Francis, Jonny Geller, Robbie Glen, Kath Grimshaw, Jack Hadley, Lisa O'Donnell, Tina Orr Munro, Loraine Peck, Veena Sankar, Clive Seale, Charlie Tyler, Emma Warrington, Gordon Wise, James Blatch, Mark Dawson, and to the many others who have taught, encouraged, and inspired.

Printed in Great Britain
by Amazon

83718058R00154